EASY COME, EASY GO

A BOMBER HANSON MYSTERY

DAVID CHAMPION

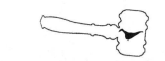

ALLEN A. KNOLL, PUBLISHERS

SANTA BARBARA, CA

Allen A. Knoll, Publishers, 200 West Victoria Street,
Santa Barbara, CA 93101
tel (805) 564-3377   fax (805) 966-6657
email: bookinfo@knollpublishers.com
website: www.knollpublishers.com

First Edition

08 07 06 05 04   5 4 3 2 1

Library of Congress Cataloging-in-Publication Data

Champion, David.
  Easy come, easy go : a Bomber Hanson mystery / David Champion.--1st ed.
     p. cm.
  ISBN 1-888310-89-8 (alk. paper)
     1. Hanson, Bomber (Fictitious character)--Fiction. 2. Women physicians--Fiction. 3.
Fathers and sons--Fiction. 4. Trials (Murder)--Fiction. 5. California--Fiction. 6.
Widows--Fiction. I. Title.

PS3553.H2649E17 2004
813'.54--dc22

                                    2003065826

Printed by Sheridan books in Chelsea, MI
Text typeface is Caslon Old Face, 12 point
Smyth sewn case bind with Skivertex Series 1 cloth

Also By David Champion

She Died for her Sins
Too Rich and Too Thin
Phantom Virus
Celebrity Trouble
Nobody Roots for Goliath
The Mountain Massacres
The Snatch

She was just a wisp of a thing—blond, pageboy haircut, thin as a rail. She looked like something you wanted to take home to a warm shelter and a good meal, like a stray calico cat perhaps. She looked like a lot of things, but not what she was—a doctor on trial for murdering her husband.

She was on the witness stand now, in a preliminary hearing. Bomber was not her lawyer—she had wanted him, but he didn't believe her story. I was in the audience at the doctor's request, not Bomber's, though I told her I would be the last person whose advice Bomber would take. Do fathers ever listen to their sons?

I believed her, but then, how could you not? She was so helpless looking. And she was nervous on the stand, which didn't help her cause. But how could you not be nervous on trial for your life?

"Easy" was what they called her late husband around town. Probably because he was uptight, and it was the only way folks could get back at him. He was like a scrub jay, beautiful and vicious. He'd taken financial advantage of practically everybody in town while he piled dollar on dollar—so high you couldn't see the top of the pile. He was rich, rich, rich, until he lost it all when the stock market sank and things caught up with him. He was captain of the ship, but he took the whole crew down with him, after he looted his stock fund under the guise of a performance bonus to the tune of untold millions of cool bucks.

Melissa, the doctor, was a general practitioner—family

practice, beloved in town when she'd married him. Nobody knew what she saw in him. Perhaps it was just the money. Doctors don't make what they used to, and she'd recently gone on salary at the big clinic in town. And he was darn handsome, there's no getting away from that. And she was nicely into her thirties, and probably had a yen for babies, and he probably made her an offer she couldn't refuse.

Easy's real name was Fred Noggle. His ancestors had made a bundle in athletic equipment, and the heirs were nice enough to hand over a healthy portion to Fred.

Fred, or Easy, was not a man devoted to patience and study. He found some gimmicks in the financial markets and pursued them with a vengeance. He claimed he had a guru stashed away in a neighboring town, and he called him a savant, so uncanny had he been with his stock market picks. What no one seemed to realize was this savant was working his magic picking stocks at a time a blind man could pick winners throwing darts at a list of Chinese stock listings.

After Easy was returned to the earth, one of the less reverent among the constabulary was overheard to say, "Easy come, Easy go." The double entendre was recognized by a few who realized his riches had come to him easily and then evaporated just as easily.

It must be confessed in my account of Bomber's trial against big tobacco, under the title *Nobody Roots for Goliath*, there was a lawyer, on our side, nicknamed Easy. He was quite a different kettle of fish from Easy Noggle. I could have changed the name but thought accuracy was more important. I think we can all be grateful the title of this book is not *Effortlessly Come, Effortlessly Go*.

District Attorney Webster Arlington Grainger III was handling the case personally. If Melissa had been an Hispanic schoolteacher or secretary that had blown away her husband, the D.A. would have been nowhere near the scene. But a *doctor* wasting a wealthy tycoon was big ticket stuff in the limited newspaper circles of Angelton, California, up the coast from Los

Angeles or down the coast from San Francisco, depending on your perspective and/or prejudices. Such was the sensational nature of the case those two metropolises were giving generous news coverage, and District Attorney Webster Grainger III was a soft touch for publicity. He liked being district attorney. He accepted the mediocre salary as his own little *pro bono publico*—his contribution to society. Webster A. Grainger was a trust fund baby—not zillions, like some around here, but enough to keep him out of the homeless shelter and insulate him from getting an honest job. Bomber always said Web was in it for the fame, not the fortune.

It was my father, Bomber Hanson, whom everybody wanted when they got in a major fix as Melissa McHagarty had. But he couldn't begin to satisfy all the supplicants, so great was the demand. One of Bomber's quirks was that he stayed small and personal. He wasn't cut out for managing a 100-lawyer firm, though sometimes I thought we could keep them all busy.

So it was just Bomber and me—and I didn't try cases, I just did investigation mostly—and Airhead, the secretary, of course. No census of the nuthouse would be complete without Bonnie V. Doone, whose initials didn't even begin to tell the tale.

In our last case, set down in *She Died For Her Sins*, I'd acquired a girlfriend—Joan Harding—causing my mother untold ecstasy, but causing Bonnie Doone heartburn. I don't mean to suggest Bonnie had any interest in me in that way—we both felt that would be incestuous, but me catching someone before she did ruffled her feathers and threw her nose just a little out of joint.

I met Joan in Chicago where the case took place. Joan was the secretary by day to the lawyer for the deceased. The rest of the time she was a world class fiddler who'd made a startling recording of the Beethoven concerto with the Cincinnati Orchestra. Joan had passed her violin audition with the Los Angeles Philharmonic with flying colors. Now she was off touring with them.

Dr. Melissa McHagarty had kept her maiden name for

3

professional purposes. Some said it was just an easy opportunity to disassociate herself from Easy.

She was sitting on the witness chair looking ever cognizant of the coaching her attorney had given her. He'd probably said, be relaxed and look confident—exude your innocence. She was trying, but faking it did not come naturally to her.

District Attorney Webster A. Grainger III was plying his trade.

"Now, Doctor—did you love your husband?"

"Of course," she said.

"How long were you married?"

"Almost three years."

"And how long had you known Mr. Noggle?"

"A little over a year before that."

"How did you meet?"

"He came to me as a patient."

"What was his complaint?"

"Bronchitis."

Somehow I expected a doctor to be tougher looking. Melissa looked like a strong wind would lift her right out of her chair and send her out onto the vast courthouse lawn.

"Did he tell you how he chose you as a doctor?"

"Later, yes," she said. "He said he was looking for a young, single woman."

"Why?"

She blushed. "I expect he was looking for a personal relationship."

"You expect," he pressured, "but you aren't sure?"

"He admitted as much."

One of Web's trademarks as a prosecutor was his sneer. He liked to sneer at the witness, probably in the hope of breaking some hapless soul by letting him or her and the jury know that he thought any answer he/she gave was highly suspect— even if it was only his/her name or occupation.

"Tell us about the circumstances of your late husband's death."

"I don't know about that," she said. "I wasn't involved."

It was a great answer. I would be sure to pass it on to Bomber.

"Very nice, Doctor," Webster said. "But you *were* involved. You found the body, didn't you?"

"*After* he died. I had no involvement with his death."

If I were to critique Dr. Melissa McHagarty from Bomber's standpoint, I would say the great advocate would have seen to it that the witness showed some sadness at the mention of her beloved's demise—some tears would be good if they could be produced believably. At minimum, a long, morose face would be in order. Melissa looked like the county coroner testifying dispassionately about a stranger.

"Doctor, tell us where you found Mr. Noggle, when you realized he was dead."

"He was in the living room slumped on the floor at his favorite chair. The TV was on the financial channel."

"What did you do then?"

"I tried reviving him."

"How?"

"I pounded his chest to get his heartbeat going. Then I gave him mouth to mouth resuscitation. That was when I tasted something very bitter that we later learned was poison."

Web didn't have to break her down, just show the judge he had the basis of a case, which seemed to go without saying.

"You are a medical doctor, Doctor, is that correct?" Web asked as his entry in the redundancy sweepstakes.

"Yes."

"And you are familiar with various compounds that can be and are used to poison human beings?"

"Yes, but I've never used one," she blurted.

"I didn't ask you that," Web said with a smug grin. I decided it was a good thing for me to be observing Web without Bomber around. I was able to concentrate on several aspects of his courtroom demeanor that were overshadowed when Bomber was on the scene. And I noticed Web was more prone to use

Bomber's tricks when the great man was not in the courtroom.

It was obvious Web was not a happy camper when he saw me sitting in the audience. This kind of court activity didn't usually draw flies, but the doctor and Easy were sufficiently notorious that the two newspapers were represented as well as a smattering of the legal community and a few court groupies.

But when Web saw me, his jaw dropped. He knew I could only be there on behalf of Bomber, and it was no secret around town that our fearless district attorney feared no man so much as Bomber Hanson at the defense table—*especially* in a case where Web expected to burnish his image. If Bomber got in the case, that would be a much rougher go—I'm tempted to say an impossibility, but that would be immodest, albeit accurate to date.

Dr. McHagarty's attorney of record was Kirk Carlisle—a nice enough chap in his eager thirties, but no match for Bomber. He was, at best, Melissa's second choice.

He stood by serviceably in a role not ordinarily associated with the limelight. The preliminary hearing was the district attorney's show to establish grounds to bind the defendant over for trial. The district attorney showed just enough of his hand to bring that off. The defense attorney was not obliged to show anything. His role was more or less to keep the district attorney on the straight and narrow—object to the real objectionable stuff and provide moral support. As near as I could tell he walked through the role as effectively as a well-programmed robot might have. Web got in all the real damning stuff, but there was really no way to keep it out.

She'd been alone with him. The coroner established he had died of potassium cyanide poisoning. The police determined there was no sign of forced entry or a struggle. That pretty much left the pretty woman. It hadn't taken long for the judge to put it on his calendar for trial.

The doctor was incarcerated for the duration. Lawyer Carlisle's plea for her release was eloquent enough—she'd been an eminent member of the community for many years, had many devoted patients as well as obligations, certainly no flight risk. But the judge, one Hiram Pendegrast, thought otherwise.

There was a whispered discussion between Melissa and her attorney Kirk Carlisle. He asked the judge for permission for his client to talk to me before she was taken back to the lock up.

"All right," the judge said, "Bailiff, stay with them."

I was summoned to the front of the room to talk to her. Kirk Carlisle was good enough to step out of hearing range.

Melissa leaned forward and whispered in a hoarse, desperate voice, "You've got to get me Bomber," she said. "They're going to hang this on me unless I get a miracle. Believe me, I didn't do it."

"I believe you," I said. I didn't add that Bomber didn't. I had a thing against rubbing salt in wounds.

"Can you at least get him to talk to me again?"

"I'll see what I can do," is all I could say.

I wasn't optimistic.

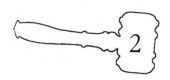

She was a widow in her thirties, not a pleasant condition. Yes, I felt sorry for her, and no, I shouldn't get personally involved with any prospective clients. Bomber was right about that.

She was so attractive, so talented and skilled a physician, and so helpless. Bomber would say I was always bringing home stray cats, and this was no different. I just couldn't let her fate hang in the hands of a second rate attorney. Could it hurt to ask a few people a couple of questions? I didn't see how.

But then, I didn't see everything.

I'm not sure what drew me back to the doctor. I'd heard her story in brief in our old Victorian house, now an office on Albert Avenue. I told Bomber I believed her. He talked to her two minutes and decided he *didn't* believe her. When she was gone he accused me of falling for a pretty face, contrary to the preponderance of evidence. I stuttered and stammered as I do with my father (and no one else), trying to explain Dr. McHagarty was not an issue since I had met the woman of my dreams. Bomber countered if he had a dime for every time I'd met the woman of my dreams he'd be close to a dollar. Humor somehow doesn't become him. Maybe I was trying to get the better of Bomber by persisting in the case of Dr. McHagarty. I really had no stake in it.

They brought the doctor into the visiting room at the jail, her arms in front of her, handcuffed. The indignity she suffered was not apparent in her carriage or on her face.

We sat across a small, desolate table from each other, and I tried to smile the smile of hope. I could see she could use

it. She poured out an embarrassing load of praise for
ing. She ended with, "I hope this means Bomber ⁊
ing…helping me."

"I wish I could say it did. I'm still going v   .
Bomber says that's the worst thing you can do. ⁊   ig
personally involved with a client. Fogs the judg   ⸴

She sank back in her chair, disappoir   g her
face. "Well," she sighed, "I guess you are be   .ng."

"And I wish that were true," I sa.   humble
experience with Bomber, my judgment is consider. ⁊ery close
to nothing."

"Now, Tod," she admonished, "this self-deprecation is
charming, but I fear it's exaggerated."

"That's very kind of you," I said, "if hopelessly optimistic. Tell me—if I asked around about what kind of guy your
late husband was, what would I hear?"

"Depends on who you talk to," she said. "His mother is
crazy about him."

"Anyone else?" I asked, looking straight at her, daring
her to include herself.

"Well…I…saw good qualities. He was very personable,
had a killer smile, could turn any girl to silly putty—a number
of men, too." She got a far off look in her eye. "He seemed to
take everything so easy—until some spark ignited his anger. He
was the picture of serenity one minute and a blazing howitzer
the next. He made his money too easy—easily, of course, but I
like easy under the circumstances."

"How did he make his first money?"

"The old fashioned way."

"Worked for it?"

"Inherited it. You might say he was living testimony to
the efficacy of the inheritance tax."

"I take it some of those good qualities faded with time
and marriage."

She answered with deliberation, "You might say that."

"Why did you marry him?"

"Oh," she said, her eyes far off again, drawing her soul back to better times. "His smile got me at first. Then it was immediately obvious to me—on talking to him—that he was a strong, take-charge kind of guy. Women like that," she said, looking at me as though she were giving me a life-enhancing tip.

"But you are an accomplished woman," I protested, "a doctor!"

"Yes, yes," she said. "When I'm a doctor I have to be strong. Mothers come in with children who have been driving them nuts, screaming all night. Or some big, burly man comes sniveling about some insignificant problem he takes to be life-threatening. Oh, I know from strong all right, but let me tell you something. I get tired of it, always having to be the strong one—always having to be interested in my patients and their problems, always trying to help them. Having a guy who took charge of *everything* was a nice change. I liked it, " she paused, then added softly, "till it became suffocating."

"So you killed him." I don't know why I said that. It was not in my nature—it just popped out.

"No," she said, her misery palpable, "I didn't kill him—but that's just what the district attorney thinks, and I suppose everybody else. Bomber doesn't believe me, does he?"

"No," I said as gently as I could. "Not yet."

She brightened at the prospect of Bomber having a change of heart.

"But you know a case might be made for justifiable homicide," I said.

"Yes, I suppose it could. Justified," she savored the word as though it were her first consideration of it.

"Like he drove you to it?" I offered in rank and transparent speculation.

She didn't answer right away but looked around for a window to look out of. There were none, and the answer did not seem to suggest itself on the walls.

When it became apparent she was not going to answer, I stepped in. "Okay," I said, "I realize I'm not Bomber, but I'm the only entrée to him. The more you can tell me, the better your shot at the big man."

"You heard my story in your office when I came begging. You heard it again in court."

"Yes," I said. "I heard the part of it you chose to tell. Young and green behind the ears as I am, I can still smell omissions. Why don't you tell me what you didn't tell in court."

She looked at me as though I were crazy. "Like what?" she asked.

"Oh, like perhaps how that potassium chloride came into your house."

"I told you. I don't know."

"Yes, you did," I said, "and I don't believe you. I'm afraid Bomber didn't believe you, and I'm sure the D.A. doesn't believe you."

She checked out the walls again.

"Look, Doctor, I'm an attorney—our conversations are privileged."

"You're not *my* attorney, and you don't practice, do you?"

"No matter. I'm a prospective attorney. I'm also not your enemy."

It didn't move her. Until I added the clincher, "Look at it this way: if you want to have the remotest chance to get Bomber to defend you, you'll have to make your case to me. Dishonesty and omissions don't go over so big with him."

She was thinking.

"Okay, look at it this way, Doctor. Can you perform your professional duties if your patients withhold information from you?"

She shook her head silently. "Okay," she said, "what have I got to lose? What part of my story do you remember?"

"All of it. He was filthy rich when you married him— from spectacular stock market gains. The market went sour. He lost a bundle—the timing of which was most unfortunate because you were in the midst of building a three-million dollar house that suddenly, mysteriously, blossomed into a *six*-million dollar house. Your husband, Easy, was a man devoted to appearance. He couldn't face financial failure—the stigma of personal failure. He had no gainful employment and living on your salary would have been a precipitous drop in lifestyle, which you say would not have bothered you, but he couldn't abide it. How am I doing so far?"

She nodded her approval.

"Okay. Out of money, Easy borrowed from some shadowy figures, and of course, trying to outsmart the stock market and recoup his losses to pay them back, also failed. The bullies closed in. Only way to save him and the house was for you to supply them with drugs. These crooks would provide the people to fill the prescriptions—all you had to do was write them. A lot of soul searching transpired and while you didn't care at all about saving the house, you did care about saving your husband, so you did it. But something kept you from continuing—conscience you say, and I'm willing to accept that for now. Easy didn't pay—you cut off the phony prescriptions, and the bad boys closed in. You say they killed him with an injection of potassium chloride. Though you don't account for how they had the expertise to do it—they aren't doctors, after all—or the access."

"They had access," she muttered. "He owed them a million—they had access. They came to the house all the time," she shuddered, and it wasn't cold. "Creeps. Like thugs in the movies. Just as sinister."

"So there they are—in your living room—in the palatial mansion, and this crook asks, 'Can you pay?' 'No,' Easy says. 'That's too bad,' he says, and takes the syringe and the poison from his pocket. 'Just going to give you a little injection. Make you rich so you can pay us.' Easy says, 'That's cool,' and holds out his arm."

"His butt," she corrected me. "They stuck it in his butt."

"Just so," I said. "Whereas you gave him vitamin injections, testosterone injections as a matter of course. He'd trust

12

you to inject him. So—there's something missing. Something big. What is it?"

She sent her eyes to the walls again—drew in a deep breath, and without looking back at me exhaled a hissing sound. "I bought the potassium. I had the needle."

"Why?"

"I was going to kill him," she said. "That's why." She spoke surprisingly matter-of-factly now, and as the burden lifted, she seemed to regenerate to her old, upbeat self.

"But you didn't kill him, you said?"

"No."

"Why not?"

"I lost my nerve," she said.

"Or someone beat you to it?"

"Yeah, they did, but I'd decided against it."

"Sure?"

She didn't answer right away. "Well," she said at last, "I think so, but that's moot now anyway, isn't it?"

"I suppose it is," I said.

She looked like she was on the verge of volunteering something else that she thought better of when the matron came in to take the doc back to the lockup.

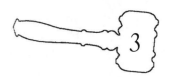

3

It was lunchtime, and I decided to meander over to the Hazelton Medical Clinic where Dr. McHagarty was most recently employed. It was a five story building—large for Angelton—with doctors packed in like sardines, catering to the medical needs and imaginations of the populace.

I found Dr. McHagarty's receptionist on the third floor, tending an empty office.

She was Stephanie Scott, she informed me with a face flooded with relief at seeing a human being on her regular shift. She wore the regulation baby blue smock that set the staff apart from the patients.

"Been quiet around here, has it?"

"Oh, my," she rolled her eyes. "Cemeteryville. I mean, it isn't exactly a secret the doctor's..." she fished for the right word, "incarcerated," she settled on at last. "Injustice of injustices."

"Don't think she did it?"

"The doctor? No way," she frowned. "I mean, if he'd been my husband I'd a done him in long ago." Unconsciously she fluffed up her dyed red hair.

"Bad apple?"

"Rotten."

"Who around here was closest to the doctor?"

"That would be me," she said without undue modesty.

"Second?"

She frowned. "Hard to say. She was friendly with a lot

of doctors. She was kind to the drug salesmen. A lot of doctors just cut them off—have no time whatsoever for them, you know?"

"Any favorite salesman?"

She was thinking, I'll say that for her. "Well…I…I…I…maybe Henry Ziggenfoos—he came around a lot. She always was real nice to him."

"Close?"

"What? Close as in romance? She was married—and to the richest, biggest hunk in town."

"Liked his looks, did you?"

"Ummm…" she fairly swooned. "I mean, that was undisputed." She looked at me puzzled, as though she expected a response. "You didn't think he was handsome?"

"Well, I never saw him."

"Oh."

"You see a lot of him?"

She made a sour face. "*Way* too much."

"In here?"

She nodded. "He was only using her if you ask me, and since you came around I guess you're asking."

I nodded, sober and somber. It was all she needed.

"It was like he didn't want her to be alone, he was always underfoot. Needed a job if you ask me. Something to occupy his time. He couldn't wait to pop the question."

"Why do you think he…popped the question?"

"Why? I *know* why. He was a money man. One of those guys who sat by the internet trading stocks, making money until the cows came home. He was getting richer by the minute if you can imagine. Lot of rich guys can't spend—so focused on making money—but not Easy. The hundred plus grand Mercedes to keep his 200 g Ferrari company—the boat too big to dock anywhere, then he built this mansion up in the hills—more millions than I can imagine. Then suddenly he lost it all. It was like all his money was being sucked into one of those black holes in space. Now the doc starts to look real good to him. None of us caught on—much less the doctor. He was marrying a meal ticket! Soon as they tied the knot he started to swagger and bluster. He had all the charm of a one-legged elephant. But," she said dreamily, "oh, that smile."

"What do you think finally broke the bank?"

"Oh, the house, for sure. You should see it."

"I'd like to."

"Half acre under roof. The finest appointments money can buy. It cost six million, *easy*."

"But how could a doctor pay that kind of mortgage?"

"Exactly!" she said. "She couldn't. Not without the hanky panky."

"What was that?"

"Ask the drug salesman."

"Henry?"

"That's him."

"How do you get hold of him?"

"I have his cell number—here," she pawed through a rolodex and recited a number which I duly wrote down.

*   *   *

Henry Ziggenfoos was not a handsome guy in the Easy Noggle sense. With thinning brown hair and teeth not too straight, he was solidly built with a touch more belly than would qualify him for a Chippendale dancer. He was nonetheless a pleasant appearing panda bear. His office was a shared room in the back of a manufacturing facility in Oxblood, just down the coast from Angelton.

He must have seen the surprise on my face as I surveyed his ultra-modest digs—no more modest than the broom closet Bomber had given me for an office, to be sure, but at least I was alone. When I did my double take, he said, "So much for the excessive profitability of the rapacious pharmaceutical companies."

"Doctor McHagarty," I said, pronouncing the name as though I were reading it in an encyclopedia.

He didn't seem to want to talk to me, which made me suspicious. We danced around the subject of Easy Noggle and Dr. McHagarty but he didn't freeze up until I casually mentioned her large drug buy. I pressed, "How well do you know Doctor McHagarty?"

"She was a good customer—a good doctor—dedicated, caring, proficient, made house calls, would you believe? Came to my house all the way in Oxblood when my wife was sick. Refused payment, would you believe?"

"Did you supply her the drugs Easy had her buy?

He opened his mouth, then closed it again.

"Doctor McHagarty got them from you," I said, as though I knew.

When he didn't comment, I pursued the line of questioning: "Don't tell me you weren't a little suspicious with her orders jumping like that."

"Hey," he said, spreading his hands apart, "I'm a drug salesman. That's how I make my living. Turning down orders doesn't put any bread on my table."

"Weren't you afraid Doctor McHagarty was into something illegal?"

"No, I honestly couldn't believe that of her."

"How about her husband?"

He groaned softly. "Well," he said at length, "I wasn't dealing with him."

"Think she was?"

"Well…as it turned out, she was," he said. "Easy ran out of money through a combination of bad luck and stupidity and she, Melissa, Doctor McHagarty, bore the brunt of it."

"Justifiable homicide?"

"Certainly justifiable."

"If *she* did it?"

"No way," he paused, "but yes, if they find out, in spite of my belief in her, she did, it was certainly justifiable."

"Someone displeases you, you kill them?"

He squirmed in his chair. "It was more than displeasure. It was forcing her to do illegal things."

"And you were an accomplice?"

"Unknowing," he said, as though begging for a bone.

"So how many drugs did you supply?"

"I don't know. I'm just an order taker."

"Then find out. Call the bean counters, get the numbers. I'll call you tomorrow morning."

"Oh, I can't work that fast."

"Afternoon, then," I said.

That mouth of his opened and closed again. "Well," he said on the second opening, "I'll do my best."

I don't know why I thought that would be good enough.

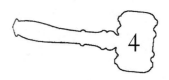

4

The mansion was up in the hills above Angelton on the up-side of Hillside Drive, in the vicinity of the first of Bomber's cases I reported in *The Mountain Massacres*. Instead of a house put together with two 20,000 gallon water tanks, it was a showplace that looked like it had been furnished out of one of those glossy catalogs that purported to purvey "things men like." I never liked any of them.

At our jailhouse meeting I had asked Dr. McHagarty for the keys to her house, but it turned out there were no keys, only combinations to key pads that opened the locks electronically. She gave me the code to the front gate and main door.

I entered the code at the main gate. Open sesame. Front door: ditto. The entry for the main living area was behind the house, where a driveway led you up to the second floor. Extra bedrooms for the non-existent kids or the speculative guests shared the downstairs with an elaborate game room.

There was the obligatory wall-to-wall television screen, poker table with the chips in a revolving container in the center. Pool table, pinball machines, table hockey and running the length of the backside wall, a regulation bowling lane. Out front on the lower level was the swimming pool and jacuzzi, with a cabana holding a sauna and wet bar. If Easy missed any amenity it was purely accidental.

The front elevation of the mansion featured a stairway wide enough for the third army to march up without ever breaking ranks.

On either side of the grand staircase were four two-story pillars that looked like they were imported from ancient Rome.

They would have warmed the heart of Donald Trump. The overall impression it gave was of the architect making fun of his client. But it could easily have been the other way around.

Self-effacement and modesty were not arrows in Easy's quiver.

I could see the Noggles having a large party with valet parking and a servant in livery directing the guests up those front steps—past the pool and spa—and hope they didn't fall in.

My first tour was cursory—see the sights, get the flavor of the place, to let myself open for inspiration.

I roamed around the main living area upstairs—the scene of the crime. This ground had already been gone over with a fine toothed comb, and nothing leaped out at me.

I headed downstairs.

For want of a plan I stumbled onto a mysterious niche in the wall behind the bowling alley, where you set up the pins. At first it looked like a convenient space to go to set up the pins after knocking them down.

A digital lock was staring me in the face, daring me to divine combinations. I tried the front gate and door combinations. No cigar. Then I tried the manufacturer's default—the number the maker sets in all his products—often 0-0-0-0 or even 1-2-3-4. I tried them all. Nothing. Easy may have been easy, but he had the gumption to program his own code.

His birthday, address and social security numbers were next, but I knew only his address. It was four digits—1441, and it didn't move those tumblers.

There was a telephone in one of those cute London bright-red phone booths, on the other end of the cavernous recreation room, and it worked. I called the Hazelton Medical Center and spoke to Dr. McHagarty's secretary. She didn't have the code info, but would endeavor to uncover it.

I drove back to the jail, and posing as the doctor's attorney got them to bring the doc out for "a couple of questions."

She seemed to be wearing down, her pallor was pale. She sat facing me.

"Do you know anything about secret closets in the house? Like the one locked behind the bowling alley?"

"Easy was big for secrets. Paranoid, obsessive. I could make a couple of new categories out of Easy, if I had a psychological bent."

"There is a combination lock on a door behind the bowling alley. Know anything...?"

She waved a hand. "Paranoia can destroy ya."

"The combo?"

"Oh, I never had any of that."

"I tried all I could guess. I could use his birthday and social security number."

"September sixth, nineteen sixty-nine," she said. I wrote it down.

"Social?"

She shook her head. "Didn't memorize it."

"Okay," I said. "Can you write two notes for me? One to your accountant asking him to give your secretary Easy's social security number."

"She will have that."

"Okay. I'll ask her. And one to whom it may concern, saying I have your permission to break into that closet, or any other space I need to investigate."

Her face clouded so dark I thought it was about to rain.

"A problem?" I asked.

"No-o-o," she said, drawing it out. "I just have visions of you demolishing the house and the D.A. thinking we were destroying evidence."

"So we'll add a note that I promise not to destroy evidence."

That seemed okay with her, so I wrote the statements on a note pad I had brought with me, and she signed them.

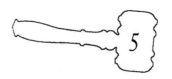

5

It was Bomber's perpetual good relations with the police that enabled me to pay a visit to the station and ask questions I could have been told were none of my business.

There were four desks in the room on the second floor of the police station on Newport Street, two of them occupied. Detective Sergeant Avery Knapp, who testified so beautifully for us in the case I reported in *She Died For Her Sins,* was at one of them. Bomber had gotten him out of a divorce fix, never a happy circumstance, with the bare minimum of agony and abuse. He had done the investigation in the Easy Noggle case. These circumstances conspired to force me, by default, into the role of questioner—not something that gels with my temperament.

We shook hands, and I sat at the chair provided at the side of his desk.

"I can't believe she did it," I began.

"Believe it," he said. "Don't get me wrong. I think it was justifiable, but no one else wielded that syringe. Who'd know how?"

"Diabetics, for one—there are millions of those."

"What's the beef?"

"Beef?" I said slapping the table with my notes. "A couple dozen swindle victims isn't beef?"

"You ever been swindled?" he asked.

"On a small scale, maybe."

He nodded—"Make you want to kill the swindler?"

"But these are big cons. Lot of money down the Easy sewer."

"Yeah, but not really anyone who couldn't afford to lose it," he said. "Funny thing about con victims—lot of them won't acknowledge they've been victimized. Fear it makes them look bad."

I nodded. I'd heard that.

"But even so…we interviewed all his suckers," he continued, "uh, customers, you know what I mean."

"You don't think any of them wanted to kill him?"

"They *all* wanted to kill him, we just couldn't tie any of them to a syringe and poison, and we couldn't figure out how Easy would have let anyone but his doctor wife stick him in the butt with a needle."

"Not a happy customer among them?"

"There was one woman who wouldn't say anything bad about him."

"Could be a cover up?"

He shrugged. "We didn't think so."

"Can I borrow the file?" I added, surprised by my own boldness.

He waved a hand. "No skin off my nose."

Surprised but happy, I took the file to a desk in an unused interrogation room. I read it carefully and made notes on a pad Avery was good enough to provide. The names, addresses and phone numbers of Easy's clients and contacts would save me a lot of legwork.

While I expected to get more or less the same tale of woe from Easy's disgruntled, I was intrigued by what the supportive woman Avery had referred to had to say. The report was customarily dry. In it she stated her belief in Easy and her feelings that the economic slump affected his speculations as adversely as it had most everyone else's. It was—or would have been, had he lived—only a temporary reversal. She had been left a bundle by a grateful husband before he went to glory. I pictured her as fairly doddering, but the report set her age at thirty-four.

When I finished gleaning all I could from his file, I went back to see Knapp. I wanted to know if they'd investigated the locked closet behind the bowling alley, but I didn't want to alert them to something they might have missed.

Back in the detective room, I eased myself into Knapp's side chair. "Thanks," I said, returning the file to his desktop, where finding a space adequate enough to hold it was not a piece of cake.

"Pleasure," he said, waving the gesture off with a loose-jointed arm.

"Find anything good at the house?" I thought I was being casual, off-handed, but his eyes froze.

"Such as?"

I didn't know if that question meant they had found something he didn't care to share or I was getting pushy and they hadn't bothered with the house.

"We gave it a once-over," he said. "But what would you expect us to find?"

"Oh, nothing in particular," I said, "a suicide note could come in handy."

He thought for a minute, then shook his head with a terse motion that put me in my place.

"Could have fifty suicide notes—you couldn't convince anyone he got that needle in him there by himself."

"So..." I prodded gently, "no surprises?"

"No surprises."

"No secrets?"

"Nah," he said. "Look," he leaned toward me as if to say, you're my pal and I'm going to level with you, "it was a straightforward murder. Often in cases like this you think you have a slamdunk, but you still have one or two dark doubts—maybe nothing big, but something." He shook his head. "Nothing this time, nothing—*nada*. This was as clean a case as we'd ever seen. Only thing make it more convincing would be a movie of the whole thing going down. The doc's a sweetheart, no? I don't blame you for being soft on her...."

I let the false accusation pass.

"And I wish she were innocent. But," he spread his hands, "too much evidence. A smart lawyer would plead justifiable homicide. Might not beat the rap, but could get a jury to agree on only putting her away for five or ten years."

"So why isn't she doing it?"

He shrugged. "Word is she's stubborn. Insists she didn't do it—isn't going to plead to a lie."

"Yeah," I said. "What would we do if we really were falsely accused?"

"I don't know—find some believable alternative," he said. "There just is nothing out there."

"And if you couldn't find anything," I pressed, "and the evidence was solid against you? You knew you didn't do it? What then?"

He set his jaw, and it looked as if he'd stopped breathing. "Two choices: try to plead out—settle for a bunch of years, or fight it on the basis of justifiable homicide and hope to get enough sympathy from the jury to get off."

"But, suppose," I said, "just suppose you *didn't* do it. Now you're faced with having to lie convincingly and consistently. And if you get tripped up—which you are bound to— you probably kiss your chances goodbye. So if you *are* innocent they could put you away for life because you screwed up at the trial."

He looked at me and nodded. "It's a cruel world," he said.

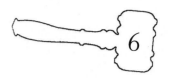

6

I can't say I wasn't sensitive about all the time I was spending extra-curricularly, so to speak, nor did I expect it to go unnoticed in the hallowed halls of the Victorian on Albert Street. But sometimes Bonnie Doone was harder to take than others.

"Well, well, well," she greeted me on that particularly gloomy, rainy morning. "Will you look what the cat dragged in!"

"Does your kindness know no bounds?"

"Listen, boy child, your *persona* has not been too very *grata* around here lately—owing perhaps to the fact that your *persona* has not *been* around here too very much lately."

"Too very much? What quaint phraseology."

"Just a friendly word of warning and a hint for you to keep your defenses up. Your daddy is trying his darndest to be understanding, but I fear the fire pouring out of his nostrils is not make believe."

So the question was, should I take Bomber-the-bull by the horns and pop in on him, flash an expansive smile, stuttering my greetings—or should I lay low and wait out the tornado? I chose the latter option, and used the time to call Henry Ziggenfoos, the drug salesman. He answered his cell phone. I could tell he didn't want to share the info about Melissa's drug purchases with me, though I reinforced that we were on her side. Even if we didn't take the case, we wouldn't be against her.

"How many?" I asked.

He told me:

A *lot*.

I was hidden away in my broom closet cum office for

less than five minutes when the walking void made her appearance in my doorway, leaned against the door jamb, and crossed her ankles and her eyes in that pose of inherent superiority which was second nature to her.

"The guy who puts his name on your paycheck in the name of charity, if truth be told, has a hankering to see you. Of course, I'd be the last to know, but I have an uncomfortable inkling that this could be his last chance."

"Why, is he sick?"

"Very funny, boy chile, very funny. I am merely speculating that if your recent inactivity around here results in a well-deserved layoff of certain investigative personnel, well, you connect the dots. Take your time."

"Thanks."

"But one more word of advice," she said with her patented supercilious air, "if you have any notion of getting out of the great man's office with your head still screwed to the rest of your body, I wouldn't dilly dally."

If there was so much urgency, I wondered, why did she waste so much time being cutesy?

I wish I could say I approached the big office with equanimity, but my heart was pounding, and this was my *father* I was going to see. I stuttered under no other circumstances, but this time I knew I'd spew spittle all over his celebrity testimonial walls if I did anything other than nod. I'm not proud of it, but there it is.

He was the Lord and Master of the shop, and he had said, "No" to Melissa McHagarty. But I wouldn't let it go. I was on my way to the man who had all the weapons, and I had no defenses.

The knock I placed on his door, if I do say so myself, was world class. Not too loud and brazen, not too soft and timid, but just right. And after all my years in his service this was not as you might suppose, automatically achieved.

I could, of course, be mistaken, but I could have sworn there was a cheery note in his voice when he said, "Come in."

And indeed after I stepped over his threshold he was beaming as though at a long lost friend just back from the Garden of Eden.

"Well, me boy, good to see you, sit down, sit down," he nodded to the chair in front of his desk.

Good to see me? the implication of that was not difficult to divine.

"Well, well," he said, still in expansive good humor, "whatchoo been up to?"

"Oh, j-j-just the u-usual."

"Usual, huh? Lot of time in the field?"

I could have played footsie with him all day and we both knew it, so I decided to take the gaff and get it over with.

"You p-p-probably know, I've b-b-been trying to g-g-get a han-handle on M-M-Melissa McHagarty's fix."

"Oh?" he raised an eyebrow. "I thought we'd turned that one down. Am I wrong?" He looked at his desk and shuffled some papers as though looking for confirmation of something he wasn't sure about.

He was sure.

In the interest of conserving spittle I nodded. Let him rant, I ought to be able to take it. But he didn't rant. He merely nodded his head. "You know," he said, "I ought to be, at a minimum, out of joint—but I'm thinking after that fine performance you put in at the courthouse on our last case, maybe you're ready to go it alone."

My jaw fell to the floor, but I wasn't so mentally deficient I wanted to respond to that one. He'd thrown me the impossible bone, and I wasn't picking it up. I just shook my head.

Now he looked shocked. "Oh, no," he said slapping his forehead too gently for a serious gesture. "You don't mean you are angling to change my mind?"

"I-I," I closed my mouth. The obvious answer was impossible and I knew it. I don't know why I turned my head to look at the floor-to-ceiling array of pictures on the wall—pictures, it seemed, of every celebrity known to man, all inscribed with extravagant praise for the great and good Bomber. Was I trying to convince myself he was right about Melissa McHagarty? How could a man with so many testimonials be wrong? Or was I more likely sending Bomber a signal—a noblesse oblige kind of thing whereby a man of his stature and celebrity owes a certain duty to those of us less endowed?

When I turned back to look at Bomber there was a disconcerting, bemused expression on his face—as though the first words out of his mouth would send me scurrying to the Salvation Army, begging to join their band.

"Tell you what," he said, and stopped.

Was something required of me?

"What?" I said.

"Take a week off. Investigate the McHagarty matter to your heart's content. You probably have some vacation coming. End of the week, come tell me what you found. Convince me I should take the case, and I'll pay you for your investigation."

"If I d-don't convince you?"

"Chalk it up to an informative vacation."

"H-how am I g-going to convince you?"

"How? Why with the facts, Boy. Find me evidence someone else done it—proof she didn't. Or you could take the other path."

"What p-path?"

"Give it up. You seem to be the only person in town who thinks the doc is innocent," he said. "Now tell the truth. Have you talked to anyone who thinks she didn't do it?"

"Yes!" I injected. "Her s-secret-tary, a drug salesman, and I've just b-begun."

"Any theories on who else could have done it? Who else could have come into his house, given him an injection at a place he couldn't reach himself without him making a fuss?"

"N-not yet."

"So you're up for the challenge? Contingency, like some of our brethren: you only get paid if you bring home the bacon?"

I was on the spot. Did I believe in Melissa that much? Sure, she'd convinced me, but was I willing to put my money where my heart was? What if I were wrong? I had so little money, sacrificing a week's pay could drive me to the poor house. Besides, I wanted to hoard my vacation time to spend with Joan when she got back from her Philharmonic tour. But something clouded my judgment.

"It's a deal," I announced.

Bomber just looked at me and cocked his head. A wry smile possessed his lips. Was he so amazed I opted to persevere under his terms, or was he simply bemused I could get three words out without stuttering?

When I stood to leave his office, he was still smiling. When I turned to walk out of the room, I could *feel* his smile burrowing into my back.

7

The game was up. I had a week. I guess that was preferable to the devious diversions I'd been taking.

Stephanie Scott called me back with Easy's social security number.

I drove my economy car back up the mountain, punched all the requisite codes in the gate and front door, then took my prospective codes to the lower floor behind the bowling alley.

I had a hunch his birthday would work, so I tried the social security number in every combination of four digits I could think of. Again, no cigar.

Easy's birthday was September sixth, nineteen-sixty-nine—so 9-6-6-9 seemed the obvious choice. As I punched the numbers with the pound or number sign first, I dreaded to think where I would turn if this didn't work. I didn't see myself kicking in the door or blasting off the hinges. I didn't want to be indicted for breaking and entering.

Hallelujah, it worked! I opened the door carefully. I had visions of some kind of alarm going off, or worse, a trapdoor springing open under me—or perhaps one of those guns rigged to fire when someone crossed the threshold.

My first shock was that I'd opened a door, not of a closet but of a rather large unfinished room with a metal desk and file cabinets, both looking like the fruits of a hard driven bargain made by Easy at a garage sale. There were papers on the desk in general disarray, and the place was thick with dust. The back wall had not been installed, so the bare dirt left from the digging of the foundations against the hill was in evidence. The floor was dirt, the other walls unfinished studs. As luxurious as the rest of the house was, this dungeon looked as if it had been planned and executed by the Marquis de Sade. Going from the house to here and back again represented big time culture shock.

I got right to work nosing around.

The desk was such a mess I decided to start with the file drawers. I was both pleased and disappointed to find the drawers unlocked. Pleased because with Easy's fetish for secrecy, I thought surely I'd have to break in—but disappointed because an unlocked drawer seemed to indicate there was nothing of interest therein.

Wrong. Virtually the first thing I pulled out was a folder marked:

Insurance Policies

The face amount—one million, his and hers, like matching towels.

Melissa hadn't mentioned the insurance. The little I know about life insurance told me Melissa had to know it existed. She would have had to sign for it. The date indicated it was less than a year old. The most obvious suspicion was that she killed him for the million.

Fishing deeper in the drawer I reeled in a fat folder entitled:

Client List

Inside was an impressive list of names both in number and throw weight—a city councilman, real estate mogul, big name actor, a number of women left well-off either by the evacuation of a husband or by his timely demise. Easy seemed especially handy with the women folk.

There were columns after the headings:

Investment Type	Payback/Date	2nd Pmt/Date	3rd Pmt/Date	Amt /Date

There was no provision for more than three payments. The only pattern I could discern was that each payment was less than the one before. The initial payment in the earlier dates was 20 to 40 percent. Those impressive numbers diminished with each subsequent payment. Some people got token payments of 10 percent or so, followed by goose eggs.

The sheets had the earmarks of a Ponzi scheme. Promise huge returns, pay them initially, then after the word gets out you are inundated with investors. Money from the new suckers goes to pay the old ones. Most often the 'investors' are so pleased with the results they let the money ride instead of taking it out, giving the schemer more to play with. All he has to do is send an official looking statement showing the original $100,000 investment had grown to $140,000 and so on. Larger "returns" were reserved for those who didn't take their money out of the fund.

The correspondence files were thick with letters—happy investors, disgruntled investors, low-key pitches, notes of encouragement to those who had apparently lost the faith.

Another file had copies of statements that were sent to the "investors." Those were apparently generated by a computer.

In the interests of truth, beauty and justice, I decided to borrow the documents—not steal, you understand—borrow. I certainly had no desire to *own* them, but the information therein might help me solve this mystery.

The file drawers didn't yield anything else of interest except a list of contacts, some of which were identified, some not. There were a lot of names and numbers which I added to my pile.

I turned to the desk. It was a mess. I am stymied by messes. Had Easy been trying to hide stuff even from himself, or was he just a mess?

There were slips of paper with phone numbers and no names, some with names and no numbers, a few names with addresses. There were also, buried deep, doodles.

One could not escape my eye. It was a crude drawing

(Easy was no artist) of what looked like a pistol being held at the head of what looked like, with a certain amount of imagination, one might construe as a woman.

Close by was a slip of paper with a distinctive name on it. Igor Sulwip. Below it in pinched writing:

Fingers

I gathered everything I could find of the slightest relevance and let myself out of the house with an armload of files and miscellany, which I would analyze at my home-apartment over the garage of a small place on the ocean. I decided against going into the office. If I was going to take a week I didn't want any interruptions.

The insurance policy was a bother. If the district attorney didn't know about it, he'd probably find out before the trial. Some people might consider a million ample motive for murder, but I still believed in Melissa. Nothing about her put me in mind of a murderess.

I was thinking about my approach to Dr. McHagarty when I let myself out the back door. I didn't want to be heavy-handed or accusative, but I wanted to get as close to the truth as possible.

I had just turned toward my car when I saw a figure slip surreptitiously around the corner of the house. My innate fear of physical confrontation made me instantly decide to hop in my car and burn rubber out of there.

I didn't see any sign of him on my way down the hill, nor did I see a vehicle of any stripe. I'd begun to think I'd imagined the intrusion until I got to the road and saw a dark, nondescript car parked under the trees.

I carefully recorded the license number. Then I realized he could have carefully recorded mine.

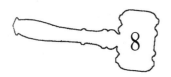

8

When I climbed the stairs with my load of files and opened the door of my garage apartment, I saw the red light blinking on my telephone answering machine. My heart always leapt at this since Joan went off to play her violin with the L.A. Philharmonic. Now that they were touring, opportunities to talk with her were not as plentiful as when she was in Los Angeles. I pushed the button and got the thrill of hearing Joan's voice.

I called her cell phone. She had her feet firmly planted in the twenty-first century. Bomber thought cell phones were an aberration. "People talking to themselves walking down the sidewalk. People talking on the phone in cars. Constant communication stifles thought. Listen to the conversation sometime. Gibberish would be too kind a judgment."

Joan didn't answer, so I left a loving message with my whereabouts.

My next call was to Officer Avery Knapp.

"Avery," I said when he came on the line, "I wonder if you could do me a big favor?"

"A favor?" he asked. "I guess as long as it isn't illegal, immoral, unethical or inconvenient."

"Just trace a license."

"Piece of cake. Give me the number."

I did.

"I'll get back to you," he said. "Regards to that impossible father of yours."

"Impossible," I said, but I wasn't sure what I meant.

The business of analyzing the data from Easy's copious

files was a time-consuming ordeal. I rounded out the first twenty-four hours of my allowed week making charts with cards hoping I could see some patterns, or have something jump out at me that would direct me straight to the case. Nothing did. I was able to get an address and/or phone number for most of his clients and contacts. My extensive resources however, did not yield any information on Igor Sulwip, a.k.a. Fingers.

I picked a couple of client names that seemed to suggest more abuse of the fiduciary relationship than seemed believable. I started with Jimmy Sherwood and Lavinia Virgil.

Jimmy lived in Angelton, Lavinia in the snotty suburb of Montelinda. So I headed for Jimmy's on the fringes of respectable Angelton. The house did not have the luxury of a family room or den, so we sat in the living room, Jimmy in one of those overstuffed reclining chairs that could jiggle your body to innumerable positions, as though being tilted just so would have some salubrious effect on the body. His chair was facing the TV set, which was on a financial channel where a serious minded fellow was bantering about stocks with the genial host. At the bottom of the screen stock quotes were speeding by.

The room had not been blessed with any touch of the female of the species, and it was not the kind of place anyone's mother would be comfortable in.

I sat in my only option—a rag-tag fugitive from someone's Boer War décor. I maneuvered the chair to face Jimmy rather than the TV. Microsoft was doing something apparently, and Verizon something else. I was always perplexed by people who made their livings making money. They didn't do anything else, performed no service for mankind, offered no lending hand to their fellow man, just dealt in stocks, bonds and currencies. Financial instruments of any stripe.

That thought put me in mind of the subject of my visit, and I said his name, "Easy Noggle."

Jimmy shot an arm out between us as though to silence me for all time on the subject. "I know why you're here," he said, his face turning sour. "Let's just not say his name."

"Okay," I said. "What can you tell me about him?"

He snorted. "Ha! What *can't* I tell you?"

"Had some financial involvement, did you?"

"Did I ever."

But he fell silent. I would have to prod, and from the look of the smoke coming out of his ears, I would have been more comfortable prodding a bull.

"Stocks and bonds?" I ventured. "Real estate?"

He frowned, and without taking his eyes from the TV, Jimmy delivered his litany.

"He was into Ponzi schemes, *par excellence*. Nobody did it better. It was a time when you only had to drop the word 'money' into any conversation anywhere and it was like flies to raw hamburger. He was usually so reluctant. The risk, the vicissitudes of the market and all. Of course people *were* getting returns of twenty-five to fifty percent a year, but past performance was no promise of future results. So okay, you'd say, can you get me a piece of it? And he didn't make them beg. He wasn't like that at all. He always managed to make room for a little more money. For, verily, the almighty buck and Easy Noggle were fast friends."

"I gather you didn't like him much?"

"You might say that."

"How did it work exactly—this Ponzi thing?"

"Lot of variations on the same theme. What's-his-name was a master, as I said. Low key, no push, no hard sell. You almost had to push *him*. Once you convinced him you seriously wanted to invest with him, he'd agree to take your money, and that was just the way it was. He was always overburdened with customers and he really didn't want any more—but, just-for-you kind of thing. So say you gave him ten grand, in a couple of months he'd give you two grand back, and you think whoa. That's like a return of eighty percent a year. You might be so excited you'd ask him to let it ride, you know, keep it, reinvest it. You can't touch that return anywhere else. But no. He wouldn't take it. Maybe next time, he'd say, 'We're making so much and so many people want in, I've got to make some disbursements.' Well, what he was saying was, 'Take the cash, sucker, it's the last you'll ever see.' You couldn't help but brag to your friends about how smart you were to make such a brilliant investment, and your friends would beg that jerk to take their money too."

"Did he pay you a referral fee?"

He shook his head, his eyes still on the TV, the sound of which I found increasingly annoying. "Didn't have to. I thought he was just doing me such a big favor letting me participate. You'd get a statement every quarter. A lot of time it would show an increase in your account of say ten percent. That works out to forty percent a year.

"On paper. After sucking you in with the first payment, he'd do the rest on paper. If you ask for the money, he'd say, 'Oh, I thought you wanted to let it ride. I got it in a company that I'm letting it ride with. But hey, anytime you want out...' I know what you're thinking—was I stupid? Yes. Was I greedy? Of course. Naïve, blind, self-deceiving—all that and more. I had a physical therapy clinic on California Street. Making a nice little bundle. But that was *work*, this was easy money," he chortled—a sore throat, rattling sound. "Easy money, yeah, yeah, in more ways than one."

"How did you discover it was a Ponzi scheme?"

"Never heard the word. Didn't know what it was. Then one day I decided to take some of my windfall out. 'Yeah, sure,' Scumbag said, 'I'll cut you a check next week when I get my dividend,' or something. I didn't pay much attention. I trusted him. Next week came, one thing or the other happened. He didn't get his dividend, and he kept putting me off—me and a couple hundred others it turned out. I went to the cops. They knew all about it. I lost my clinic. I was counting on that money to pay off some notes."

"What are you doing now?"

"I'm going to law school. Living off student loans." He smiled a rueful smile. "Signed up for law school to sue him blind, but somebody took care of him."

"Any ideas?"

"Too many ideas. They got his wife, don't they? I wouldn't blame her."

"Any idea why Easy would go in for such a swindle? I mean, he inherited a lot of money, didn't he?"

"Greed," he said, "knows no bounds." Then after a beat he added, "I should know."

"I guess that was a pretty bitter lesson in high finance."

"Yeah," he said. "Reminds me of a story that tells how I feel. There was this guy, Sam, who owed a lot of people money—so much to so many he couldn't begin to pay it back. He got depressed and wanted to kill himself. 'No, no,' his friend said, 'too drastic. Let's just pass the word you killed yourself, and put on a funeral. You can't collect from a dead man.'

"Sam thought that sounded okay. So they had the funeral and his creditors turned out in full strength. Surprisingly there was a lot of sadness and weeping. One after the other of these hard-bitten business men approached the coffin and said, 'Sam, why did you do this? Money is not worth killing yourself for. You owed me fifteen grand, but your life is worth much more than that to me. I'd have forgiven the debt if only you asked.' One after another repeated this sentiment. If only Sam hadn't killed himself they gladly would have forgotten and forgiven the debt. Until finally this little guy steps up to the coffin and says, 'Sam, you cheap chiseler, you owe me a lousy five hundred bucks, and I'm damn angry you pulled this stunt to get out of paying me. So just to make sure you're dead I'm going to stick this knife in you.' With that Sam rises up, putting out his arm to stop the knife, and says, 'Stop! *You* I'll pay!'

"If they hadn't cremated the S.O.B. I'da killed him myself."

"So if his wife did it, you'd say she was justified?"

"*Whoever* did it was justified."

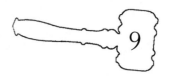

9

Contrary to most people I tried to get information from, Lavinia Virgil professed to be downright eager to talk to me about Easy Noggle. That should have made me suspicious.

I'd call Montelinda—Lavinia Virgil's section of town—the high rent district, except very few people rented there. Blue chip owners mostly. A lot of mature trees and grand houses set back discreetly from the road characterized Montelinda. Lavinia's place was a French farmhouse without the grapevines. I parked in a most commodious driveway next to a cream colored, late model Rolls Royce. Apparently she hadn't lost *everything*.

Answering the door, she displayed all the upbeat vigor she had on the phone.

With dark hair and dancing eyes, Lavinia Virgil was as attractive as Dr. Melissa McHagarty, but in a starkly contrasting way. She had one of those faces that smiled at you out of one of those local newspapers and magazines dedicated to flattering the rich. She and everyone else pictured would have a glass of happy juice in her hand and be decked out in a figure-flattering black dress.

She invited me into her decorator's dream living room, furnished in keeping with the French country house architecture. Cozy, comfy and expensive.

It was said Easy could smell money ten miles away.

We sat on facing furry loveseats with a low coffee table between us. On it were pictures of Easy Noggle in tennis attire, holding a racket as though he were about to deliver himself of a murderous backhand. There was a shiny walnut-cased grand piano in the corner. It was covered with silver framed pictures. They didn't all have Easy in them, but a lot of them did. Some with Lavinia, some without Lavinia.

Lavinia saw me looking at the pictures.

"He was a good looking man, wasn't he?"

"Hmm," I said, choosing my words carefully, "you had a...good...relationship with Easy?"

"Yes," she said, "very good."

"You didn't lose money?"

She waved a hand as though that were of no consequence. "We *all* lost money. I figure it was for a good cause."

"The cancer society?" I asked, somewhat confused.

"No, Easy. He was a good cause."

"How so?"

"Oh," she said, her eyes drifting dreamingly around her French farmhouse, then settling on the picture of Easy, the tennis ace. I wasn't going to get a straight answer to that one.

"Well," I began casually, "from the little I've heard, Easy must have been quite a guy."

She nodded silently.

Come on, I thought, loosen up, you got all these pictures of Easy around, you have to know something. Then it hit me. There could be more to this than meets the eye. But how to get it out of her was, I thought, going to take more finesse than I had. I took a stab at it. "I understand Easy was a bit of a ladies' man."

She stiffened.

"Know anything about that?"

"I wouldn't know about that," she said. "He was my investment counselor."

I nodded as though in agreement. "Must have been a good one..."

"He was," she put in quickly, before I had a chance to

finish my thought.

"...in his day."

"Everyone has reverses," she said, stoutly defending him.

"Yes," I said, the soul of understanding, "and there aren't many clients who have been burned who speak so well of the burner."

"I liked him," she admitted.

"Must have," I said, scanning the pictures with a turn of my head, "to have so many pictures of him."

I'd expected her to get angry, but she just sat there, her vision blurred with the good times that would be no more. We sat in silence for a slice of time long enough to play a Beethoven sonata—well, maybe only a second movement. Well, maybe only without repeats. It's so easy to exaggerate.

"Ever have any kind of...oh, interest...in him...other than investments?"

"Interest?" she said as though not understanding. "Isn't that an *investment* term?"

"Right," I said. "I was thinking more of a *personal* interest. Ever think he should have married you instead of Dr. McHagarty?"

"That little mouse," she said, and I would be hard pressed to say she said it nicely.

"Yes," I said, "you seem so much more...what's the female equivalent of macho?"

She let loose a short laugh. "It doesn't translate," she said. "We don't want to be sumo wrestlers. Oh, we have a few body builders; but that, frankly, is not my cup of tea. Women," she said as though instructing me in the basic art of gender, "want to be desirable—sexy, soigné, sophisticated."

"Did Easy agree?"

"Easy," she said with a short laugh, "Easy didn't know when he had it good," she said, as though her guard had fallen away, "not until he married that...*mouse!* Then he knew."

42

"And he came running back," I slipped in.

She smiled, but she didn't argue. I looked again at the pictures and at Lavinia. She was a good looking woman, no gainsaying that.

"I expect you might have been put out when he married the doctor."

She wrinkled her nose as though she were experiencing a bad odor. Her lips pursed tightly.

I waited. Nothing. "I suppose," I said more to rile her into a confession, "you might have been angry enough to...well...kill Easy for his betrayal."

She waved a hand at me as though that were the silliest notion she'd ever heard. "I don't even own a gun," she said.

Surely she knew Easy had not been shot. But I was more interested in her emotional responses than specifics. "It wasn't done with a gun," I said.

"Whatever," she said, waving another arm, which was beginning to remind me of a bird, but was it a scavenging eagle, a turkey vulture or a dove? Or perhaps a pigeon?

"Ever have any experience with syringes?"

"Syringes? As in intravenous drug use? No. Why?"

"Just wondered," I said, as though I couldn't care less. "So, when did you see Easy last?"

"The day before he died," she said, and unless I miss my guess I think she said it proudly.

My eyebrows expressed some surprise. "You continued your relationship—after he was married?"

She waved one of those wings at me. "Don't make it sound so sinister," she said. "We had...financial interests in common," she said.

"Weren't they pretty much a thing of the past at that point?"

"Oh," she said, exhaling in exasperation. "Why do you care? Our relationship was what it was. It was pure, it was mutual, it didn't die with his marriage. Had I married, it wouldn't have died with mine."

Perhaps I was old fashioned, and hopelessly so, but I couldn't just blithely accept her cavalier attitudes. But it did go a long way in explaining why she didn't hold her losses against him.

"Well, I guess all that is your business."

"Yes," she said, looking right through me as though I were cellophane and she were a smart bomb.

"But," I wondered, "you seem to have such a good attitude about Easy and your losses with him. Could you tell me how much you did lose?"

I had Easy's bookkeeping. I wanted to test it against her.

"I don't know those petty details. My account grew by leaps and bounds. I let it ride. I didn't need to nickel and dime him asking for dividends or monthly payments."

"So you have so much, the losses didn't hurt you?"

She sighed again and eased her beautiful body back in the chair. "I lost everything." That shocked me, and she knew it the way I looked around the house as if to say, will you lose the house?

"It wasn't all to Easy. I had other accounts, other bad advice, the wrong kind of stocks, risky margin purchases. Pretty much zeroed out, well you know what I always say."

"What?"

"Easy come, easy go."

"So you had other advice? Besides Easy?"

She nodded, slowly. "I guess toward the end it was pretty much Easy."

"And you never thought you were being taken advantage of?"

She shook her head. "Too many people think Easy was a crook," she said. "He wasn't. He had legitimate investments that went sour. He wasn't the only one that happened to in this market."

"What kind of investments, specifically?" I asked.

"You name it, he had it," she said. "Stocks, bonds, currency, real estate, loans and investment trusts."

"How did he manage so much?"

"He had a guru in Alameda Padre Serra up the coast. Called him a savant."

"Know where I could get in touch with him?"

"No—never met him."

"Could help clear Easy's name," I prodded.

"I don't even know his name."

"If I gave you a couple names do you think you could recognize one of them?"

She shook her head. "Easy only referred to him as 'my guru' or 'my savant.' That's all I know."

I was trying to put two and two together to get a number I recognized "Wait," I said. I thought I had it. "Stop me if I'm wrong. Easy wanted to marry you, but he'd already used all your money, so he had to go for someone who had an income."

She just looked at me through the cellophane. Bombs were no longer needed to pierce it. "But he let you know he still preferred you, and your relationship continued right up to his death."

Her eyes narrowed in anger, but she didn't argue. She stood up to terminate the interview.

"Just tell me one more thing," I said, standing to accommodate her wishes.

She cocked her head in challenge.

"Did Melissa McHagarty know about your affair?"

There was a long silence as she led me to the door. I considered not following her, but such ungraciousness was not in my nature. She opened the door.

"Thank you for seeing me," I said.

She nodded curtly. Just before she shut the door, Lavinia Virgil said, "She knew."

10

Back in my lair above the old woman's garage on the beach in Angelton, I went carefully through the papers I had collected in Easy's secret office. I was looking for the guru, but nothing popped out of the myriad of names and numbers. I isolated those with the Alameda Padre Serra telephone prefixes. There were four of them. Two were women. I reasoned Easy's guru had to be a man. I don't know why.

I cross-referenced the names with the Alameda Padre Serra phone book, which I got in the library, and one of the names owned a tire store. I decided to chance the other—a man with a personal listing in the phone book. I thought his name, Ossip Quigley, lent itself to gurudom.

It was one of those instances when I thought a telephone call might have been counterproductive. So I headed my car up the coast—a car held, no doubt, in high esteem by the frugal set.

It was a delightful college town with just the right number of people on the streets. No hustle-bustle, no hurly-burly, just a lilt with a heartwarming ambiance.

I had never been on the outskirts of Alameda Padre Serra where my map directed me in search of Ossip Quigley's address. The fairyland ambiance of the downtown did not carry through to Ossip's neighborhood, which suffered the curse of the California tract. This particular tract was not at the upper end of the scale. Several of the yards were unkempt. All the houses were squat, one-story jobs, many in sore want of upkeep.

But when I turned the corner onto the address I had for Ossip Quigley and spied his shack on the left, all other houses in the neighborhood seemed luxurious by comparison.

Guru? Savant? Well, I supposed some of them were eccentric.

The yard gave evidence, albeit scant, that there had once flourished there a lawn. The garage took up most of the left half of the front yard. The other side hosted an old car up on blocks, only one wheel still intact. My first impression was that it could pass, in some venues, as a modern sculpture. Somehow I didn't think the neighbors thought so.

The garage door was full of holes, slats were missing; wood add-ons, applied to stucco to give the house a touch of design, had warped from lack of waterproof paint, and had loosed their moorings.

With no lack of trepidation I put a finger to the doorbell and pressed. No response—probably because, like the car, the doorbell no longer functioned.

I knocked.

"Come in!" barked a male voice that didn't seem accustomed to barking.

Gingerly I opened the door, and as soon as I did I found myself discombobulated in the semidarkness of a junkyard. When my eyes acclimated I couldn't find the occupant. The windows that weren't broken and boarded up with plywood had shades drawn against the light. There was the muffled sound of a radio or TV coming from somewhere.

My eyes glommed onto the kitchen first. It was on the right of the entry and featured a motorcycle without a seat propped against a refrigerator and a bicycle with a missing wheel lying on the kitchen table on top of a myriad of papers, but no person to go with the voice. I really had no desire to venture too far into this "house" with its problematic environment. If I ever found Quigley I vowed I would not ask him to see the rest of the house. And just to be prudent I was keeping my back to the wall. My big hope at the moment was that I would not have to go to the bathroom.

I peered into the living room and almost fainted at what I saw. There amid the characteristic rubble hung a slab of meat.

It was when the side of beef said, "What do you want?" that I realized I'd found my prey, and he was hanging by his ankles from a steel bar attached to the ceiling. His eyes were straight ahead.

"Mister Ossip Quigley?" I asked, an embarrassing tremor in my voice.

"What do you want?" was the only acknowledgement I got.

Before I could answer, I stepped closer into the room where Ossip Quigley hung by his feet from the ceiling and saw he was staring at a peculiar apparatus—peculiar, I noticed, because it was an upside down TV.

"Oh," I said, looking from the back of the TV to his upside down face with its graying moustache and flaccid skin.

He didn't seem to be making any effort to right himself.

"Is this a health thing?" I said, waving at his inverted body.

"A moron could tell that," he said. "All the weight we carry on our backbones makes those disks compress. I'm giving my spine a rest from gravity. You should try it."

"Yeah—well, maybe I will."

Genius explains a lot, I thought. When one segment of the brain is so highly developed other facets of life often get blocked out. Of course I was relying on hearsay that this man was a genius. I suspected he was simply a kook. Either way, he showed no sign of righting himself.

"What do you want?" he repeated.

"Easy Noggle," I said.

"He's dead," he said.

"So I'm told," I said. "Know anything about it?"

He shook his head, which seemed to take some doing upside down. "Don't tell me you're here for that wife of his."

"Well, in a way."

"She drives me nuts."

"Oh—" that surprised me. "You know her?"

"Know her? I can't get rid of her."

"I don't follow you."

"No? Suppose you tell me what your interest is in Easy? Now that he's gone."

"I'm investigating his murder."

"You're a cop?"

"His widow wants Bomber Hanson to defend her. I'm investigating for him."

"Well, I got nothing to tell you. They arrest that wife of his it'll be the happiest day of my life."

"Count your blessings then. She's in jail."

"What're you talking about? How long's she been in jail?"

"Couple weeks."

"Oh no—she was just here yesterday."

"Easy Noggle's wife?"

"The same."

"Doctor McHagarty?"

"Who? Ursula York—driving me nuts. Thinks she has money coming. I don't owe her diddly."

Trying not to lose momentum by reacting to *that* bomb, I merely said, "Oh, why does she think you owe her money?"

"Tied me up with Easy. A mixed blessing I can tell you. Has this stupid notion I owe her a percentage."

"How did she know you?"

"Mutual friend," he said with an air of mystery.

"When were they married?"

"I don't know—seems she's been bugging me for years—five, six?"

"When did you start 'advising' Easy? That's what you did, I take it, give him investment advice?"

"About five years ago, maybe less."

"How did he pay you?"

"Slowly—if at all."

"Based on what?"

"A fee at first—then one percent of his gains. Very modest, but it could have been fifty percent for all I saw of it."

"So he was actually making investments?"

"Couldn't prove it by me," he said, dangling from his feet.

"Did Ms. York realize Easy had married again?"

"Realized, perhaps. Accepted? Never."

"Don't we call that bigamy?"

"Uh huh. Easy didn't miss a trick if there was money attached."

I looked around the trashed room for some sign of his profession.

"Can you tell me where to find Ms. York?"

"Find her? Stick around and she'll find you. Hardly a day goes by without that nuisance sticking her head in here."

"Lives around here?"

"Couple blocks."

That put me off my feed. I wanted to blurt out, I thought that you said she was *rich!* But that would be indelicate. Guru Quigley read my mind, perhaps from the dropping of my jaw. "Used to live on a huge ranch in the valley. Easy cleaned her out."

"But why didn't he just divorce her?"

"Too much trouble for Easy, and he couldn't stand anyone peeking at his finances. Now we know why."

"How did you fit into his operation?" I asked.

"I told you, I gave him investment advice—the world markets."

"What did he do with the advice?"

"I guess no one knows the answer to that besides Easy."

"Any ideas? Speculations?"

"He was selling shares in a mutual fund. Stocks and bonds—supposed to be balanced. I gave him tips. He bought shares and bonds for the fund."

"But you don't know if he actually bought anything. If there even *was* a fund?"

"No. I gave advice only. What he did with it was up to him."

"Any of his customers call you direct? Check on your advice?"

"Oh no. Easy wouldn't give my number *or* name to anyone."

"But Ms. York knew you were helping him?"

"Unfortunately."

"Where did you get your information on what to recommend?"

"A lifetime of study."

"Of the markets?"

"Of human nature."

"Any training in stocks, bonds, arbitrage, any markets, banking, financing?"

"Those birds don't know anything. Markets are fueled by people and their emotions. To understand the markets you have to understand people."

I nodded. "I imagine that's true, but how do you quantify that?"

"That's my particular expertise."

"Do you chart stocks—check formations for signals of future price movements?"

"Ah," he said. "Voodoo."

"So what do you do?"

"I told you. I study human nature."

"Hanging upside down in your living room, watching TV on an upside down set?"

"It's the same plane I'm in. Can you give me a better source for studying in depth the follies and foibles of mankind?"

"Perhaps not, I just don't see how you can translate anything you see on TV into stock tips. Do you watch the money channels?"

"Never. Charlatans! Easiest and quickest way to go broke is with their advice."

"Some might say Easy went broke taking your advice."

"They would be in error. I gave only solid, realistic, practical and pragmatic advice."

"What?" I said, losing patience. "Specifically, what advice did you give Easy about investments?"

"You wouldn't understand."

"Try me."

"You haven't got the karma."

"Look, Mister Quigley, Easy is dead. His last wife is accused. It's serious business. Your evasive answers could send an innocent woman to the gas chamber," I exaggerated a bit, my anger getting the better of me.

"I'm not about any narrow considerations. When I *feel* good about a stock, I say so. I must say I've felt good about some real winners, but I don't think you'd understand that."

"Any *losers?* Ever feel real good about any losers?"

"Losers, winners, they can be the same," he said waving an upside down arm to show how little he thought of my questions.

It finally occurred to me this Ossip Quigley was pure and simple a charlatan, but I don't think Easy cared. I was wasting my time.

"Well, thanks for your time," I said. "Want me to help you get down?"

"*Down?* Why? You should hang by your ankles, kid. Do you some good. Clears the brain of the superficial thought processes."

"So I could give stock tips too—watching Oprah?"

"Could do a lot worse, kid," he said, and I think he winked at me.

"Where can I find Ursula York?"

"Up the street to Magnolia two blocks. Turn left. Second house on the right."

"Number?"

"I'm sure it has one," his eye twitching in that quasi wink again, but I couldn't be sure since he was hanging upside down.

Ursula was well named. Wagnerian in stature with the requisite bleached straw hair and a carriage that could have displaced any number of Valkyries.

When I told her Ossip Quigley had sent me, she sighed in exasperation, but opened the screen door to admit me.

"Don't believe *anything* he says," she started in as I was following her to her frumpy living room.

She put me in mind of low brass—tubas, trombones—and a few French horns at the lower reaches of their registers.

"Says you bug him all the time."

She snorted a super snort that demanded to be reckoned with. "I'm keeping him alive. How far did you get into the place?"

"Too far," I said.

"Of course, silly question. He wouldn't *eat* if I didn't go over there. I don't know why I bother. He struggles to be a curmudgeon but underneath he's a pussy cat."

"Any reason he might want to kill Easy Noggle?"

"Hah! You saw him—Easy would have to come to his rat cage and bring the means. Ossip Quigley is without gumption. Now me—I'd have reason to kill him."

"What's that?"

"He cleaned me out. I was a woman of means—now look at me," she said, spreading her hands around the room. "Left me for another gold mine."

"I don't think Doctor McHagarty has a lot of money.

She has a job."

"Whatever. Maybe he married a doctor to boost his status. All I know is he cleaned me out, then he *dumped* me."

"What else can you tell me about Easy Noggle?"

"You might say things came easy to Easy." She spoke simply, as though the recitation were a staple in her repertoire. "He was born to a wealthy manufacturing family with not a lot of parental attention, but apparently some loving nannies. I don't think he ever learned to consider other people—their needs and feelings. I certainly never saw any evidence of it."

"Any siblings?"

"An older brother who went into the family business and a younger sister who was the apple of everybody's eye—except Easy's, apparently."

"Could Easy have gone into the family business?"

"He always said he could have. It was his choice not to. But I'm not so sure."

"How so?"

"I got the impression that it was his father's choice to have his older brother, and there was no other meaningful spot for Easy. I think he resented that slight and spent his life trying to show he could make even more money than his brother."

"Where did he get the money to start?"

"Some buyout of his share of the family business. Told them he didn't want to wait until they were all dead—or something similarly charming. My understanding is he took a lot less than he was due."

"Any idea how much?"

"He never told me, but my sense of it after putting together all I knew was that it was millions, but not tens of millions. If he had waited it could easily have been hundreds of millions."

"Was he glad he sold out?"

"Easy was never glad about any transaction. He always wanted more. He would have liked it both ways—a nice nest egg to start and the pot of gold at the end of the rainbow. By the time I met Easy, he'd gone through most of it. Hence, my appeal."

"How did you meet?"

"Mutual friend—another patsy. She said, 'He's handsome, charming, rich, and what's more he'll make *you* rich. He's doubled our money in less than three years.'"

"Did you ever meet Doctor McHagarty?"

"Did I ever!" Ursula answered with gusto. "A friend told me she saw him acting—how did she put it—attentive? solicitous? to this young blond woman—squiring her about town. When I confronted Easy, he said, 'Oh, no, that's just my doctor.' I said, 'What's wrong with you—you need a doctor?' He had a hard time with that one. Came up with bad back or something, I recall. Coming to think of it, that's how Ossip Quigley got out of Vietnam and got his pathetic little pension. Bad back! Not traceable by the most modern equipment. Not verifiable."

"So you had an altercation with Melissa McHagarty?"

"You might say that," she said, "if you were given to understatement."

"Can you tell me about it?"

"Well, I wasn't born yesterday—I could see what was happening and what was going on. All I had to do to track her down was peek at Easy's calendar. He had so many appointments with Doctor McHagarty—you'd think he was suffering from terminal cancer. Well, I planned it so I'd arrive at the doctor's office during his next appointment—confront them both at the same time.

"I got there and a receptionist said, 'The doctor is out to lunch.' I waited. When I saw them out the window holding hands, I lost it. I met them just as they came into the building, and I guess I must have made an awful fuss because they had to get the building security to restrain me. Well, now Doctor McHagarty's in jail and I'm sorry. But it's not as though she went into it blindly. That night Easy didn't come home—it was my ranch we were living on, and it couldn't have been more than two or three weeks after that I got a notice of foreclosure. I'd owned it free and clear, but Easy took out a huge loan which he said he would pay, and of course I don't have to tell you, he never did."

"And you never divorced?"

She shook her head. "I thought, what do I need a divorce for, I can't afford a lawyer, and Easy had nothing to give me by that time."

"How do you live?"

"Frugally," she said. "I work part time at the jewelry store a friend of mine from my more prosperous days owns. I do a little babysitting, and Ossip gives me a little for looking out for him."

The sun had lost its interest in Ursula's little house, finding, no doubt, more interesting company elsewhere. I thought Ursula might turn on some lights, but she didn't.

"So, in hindsight, what do you think of Easy?"

"I can't stand him. Hate is such a strong word, but there's a guy I wouldn't shy from using it on."

"Hate him enough to kill him?"

"Good God, no. In the end not only could I not stand Easy, he couldn't stand me. He wouldn't let me in the door."

"How about if he thought you were bringing him money?"

"Pugh!" she splattered. "He knew he'd milked this old cow dry, don't you worry about that. If I'd had any money left we'd still be married."

"Would you have liked that?"

Her nose seemed to develop an itch, which she tried to soothe by wiggling it. "I liked him when he was attentive, but it didn't last longer than it took for him to get all my money."

"Had considerable, did you?"

"Considerable," she said.

It was not an invitation to further inquiry. I stood to leave. She stood too.

"It was nice talking to you," I said, and I could see that pleased her. "Oh, by the way, where might I find Easy's first wife?"

"In the graveyard," she said, cocking an eye in my direction. "Domestic accident of some sort. Easy's story was she was a drinker and fell down the stairs."

"You think he pushed her?"

"Crossed my mind."

"Did he inherit?"

"Got the insurance payoff."

"What was her name?"

"Isabel."

"Isabel what?"

"Noggle, of course."

"Maiden name?"

"'Fraid I didn't know her then. But she had a brother, something of a redneck, Easy told me."

"Know his name?"

"Afraid not. But Easy and she lived on the outskirts of Angelton. Maybe you can find a marriage license or something."

"Yeah," I said. "Thanks. If anything further occurs to you, I hope you'll call."

"I will," she said.

I knew she wouldn't.

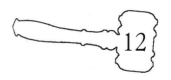

12

Perhaps someday I would become sufficiently less unthreatening so people would not be so free with the advice on how to do my job.

But the marriage license bureau was not a bad suggestion. I just tried to get the information quicker and easier, so I called Easy's girlfriend Lavinia.

She fairly purred into the phone. The kittenish pose was to let me know that she and Easy went *way* back—yes, as far as Isabel, his first wife.

"Xeres," she said, "isn't that some name?"

"Had a brother, did she?"

"She did. An unpleasant sort. I'm afraid I've repressed the name at the moment, but it'll come to me. Lives down the coast somewhere. Works in town for one of those concerns that clear drains."

"Rooter. Roto Rooter."

"Something like that. Maybe if I consulted the phone book it would jog my memory," she said. "Hang on a minute."

I heard the phone being put down on a hard surface. Then the sound of pages turning rapidly at first, then more slowly.

"God, there are a lot of them," she said. "Like auto body repair—recession-proof. Sewers, septic tanks. We'll get to the bottom of it, don't worry."

I laughed. I thought she meant that to be funny. I didn't hear any laughter from her end.

"Here it is. I think this is it. Smiley's Rooter on Harrison," and she gave me the phone number. "Still can't think of his first name, though," she said. "But there won't be more than one Xeres there."

I thanked her profusely.

"Don't mention it," she said. "Keep in touch."

I called Smiley's and a man answered who couldn't have been smiley.

"You have a Mister Xeres there?" I asked.

"What's the beef?" he answered with a question, gruff as a grizzly bear.

"You Xeres?"

"You gotta pipe need reaming? Somethin' not done right?"

"No. I'd just like to talk to Mister Xeres."

"What you think you been doing, playing tiddley winks?" he asked. "And it's Billy Bob."

"Oh, Billy Bob, I'm Tod Hanson, I'm an investigator working on the murder of Easy Noggle." There was a groan from Xeres' end of the phone. "Could we meet to talk about it?"

"All I know about it is it was the happiest day of my life when I heard."

"Wasn't he married to your sister?"

"Till he killed her."

"I would be grateful for a few minutes of your time."

"Okay, I get off at four. I'll let you buy me one. Know Henry's Bar?"

"On fourth?"

"I'll see you there. Bring money. I may feel like having more than one. Just thinking about Easy does that to me."

That suited me. In my experience, the more a person drank, the more he told.

I got to the bar twenty minutes early and ordered a ginger ale. "Will you put that in a beer mug, please?"

The bartender, a husky woman with a touch of the Y chromosome, looked at me with a cocked eye. "Trying to look grown up?" she asked.

"Exactly," I said. "And here," I produced two twenty dollar bills. "I'm going to have a guest. Take what he drinks out of that. If it goes over, I'll make it up when he leaves."

She kept her eyes on me as she absorbed the bills—not so much with her hand but her whole body.

"Our secret," I said weakly. If Billy Bob picked the place, they probably knew each other.

As far as I could see there was nothing unusual about the bar except the bartender. There was nothing high end about the place—well worn naugahyde maroon bar stools—the bar had swimming pool coping and the floor was standard barn planks.

Two minutes after four, Billy Bob came hoofing over those planks. I had no doubt it was he. Some people just *look* their voice, and he was one of them.

"Ted," he grunted, slipping into the stool beside me.

"Tod," I said, putting out my hand. He had a bone crushing shake, of which if the grin on his face was any indication, he was inordinately proud. I don't think my correcting of his pronouncing of my name registered.

Billy Bob had a full red beard and shaggy hair to match. He was short, muscular and squat—not a guy you'd mess with. I wouldn't have given Easy two minutes in a bout with Billy Bob.

"What can I get you?" the barkeeper asked—throwing a napkin down in front of him.

Billy Bob looked at my drink. "Shall I have what he's having, or the usual?" he asked, not expecting an answer.

She gave it to him anyway. "The usual," she said, to my everlasting relief.

"Yes, well, okay," he said, waving his hand at her and turning to me. "What's your connection to the late, unlamented Easy Noggle?"

"I'm investigating his murder."

"For the cops?"

"For Bomber Hanson, the attorney."

I was happy to see that name registered, and he was impressed.

"He's representing the doctor?"

"Not yet," I said. "Still working on it."

"Get her off. I couldn't be happier he's gone."

"Do I get your drift? You weren't sorry he bought it?"

The bartender sat a beer in front of Billy Bob—he took a healthy (or *unhealthy,* as the case may be) swig.

"Hey, I'd kill the S.O.B. if he weren't dead. I was practically devoting my life to that end when someone else got him."

"What were you waiting for?"

"I had this funny idea I could move the slow wheels of justice. I hounded the D.A., but I think he was in bed with Easy."

"In bed? How do you mean?"

"I'll bet anything the D.A. was investing with him. Easy's a hot potato. D.A. starts making waves, someone is sure to pick up on how foolish Mister D.A. was himself."

"So if you hadn't succeeded with the D.A. you would have killed Easy?"

"You bet I would! He killed my little sister. I don't like the phrase getting away with murder. I adored my little sister." His eyes clouded over.

"So did I," I mumbled.

"You knew her?" his eyes did the surprise trick.

"Sorry. I was talking of my sister."

"Dead?"

I nodded.

"Murdered?"

"Suicide."

"Oh, that's too bad."

"Couldn't cope. Had a wilted hand. No boyfriends."

"Isabel, my sis, was gorgeous—to a fault."

"How did she get hooked up with Easy Noggle?"

"She was waitressing and he came on to her. Had all kinds of money. What can I say? He knocked her off her feet—

61

in more ways than one. I couldn't be happier he's dead."

He drained his beer. I signaled the barkeeper for another. She set it on front of him. From the look of Billy Bob, Easy didn't pick Isabel out of any debutante lineup.

"Sure you didn't do it? Justifiably...?"

"Naw. An injection's too easy on him. I'd a split his head open with a meat axe. Even that would have been too good for the bum that killed my sis."

He didn't say bum exactly. I have done a heavy job of sanitizing his speech. His English seemed built on some sturdy, if overused, profanity.

"So what happened?" I asked.

"He made a play for her—with malice aforethought." Billy Bob spoke to let you know he knew some biggies, but when looked at closely, most of his more esoteric phrases owed their origin to TV, and he misunderstood the context.

"Took out a huge insurance policy on her, then pushed her down the steps."

"Could she have fallen? An accident?"

"If that was an accident, I'm Aunt Jemima. Easy would do *anything* for money. The easier he got it, the better he liked it."

"But...wasn't she a strong young woman?"

He looked at me as though I were crazy.

"I mean were there signs of struggle? Lot of people fall down the steps without dying. Seems to me the only ones who die are frail old people. And if she *didn't* die he could be faced with an attempted murder rap."

"B.S.," he said. "You didn't know Isabel. Isabel was no G.D. drinker. Maybe order a beer sometimes to be sociable—wouldn't drink half of it. When she...died...she was swimming in effing alcohol."

"What do you think?"

"I don't think, I effing know. *He* got that booze in her if he had to do *that* with a syringe."

"Did Easy collect on the insurance?"

"You bet your behind he did. He had it all figured out in the beginning. It was his *modus operandi.*"

"But…didn't the insurance company investigate?"

"Nah. The cops did, but they said it was an accident."

"In bed with the cops too?" I asked, skeptical that was the case.

"I'm telling you, you don't *know* Easy. He's got all these money schemes. Probably seemed effing legit at the time. It's just coming out now that he's dead it was all phony. He'd *invest* it for the cops. Double their money in a year. Not bad. He used the insurance payoff to double their money. Man, money is *everything*. Easy knew that, it didn't take a genius. Now you get the idea why the cops said it was an accident? Why that prissy D.A. didn't go after Easy?"

"I don't know, Billy Bob. You're talking bribery. That's a serious charge. I know District Attorney Grainger. I don't think he'd cover up a murder."

"Moot now," he said, guzzling his beer. I got him another.

"Maybe not moot," I said, wondering if he knew what moot meant.

"Moot!" he insisted. "Easy got his million, and…"

"A million?" Same as Dr. McHagarty's policy. For that kind of dough, I thought, the insurance company *would* do some checking. But according to Billy Bob, they hadn't.

I thanked Billy Bob for his help and risked another hand injury by sticking my mitt out. He obliged with a display of Olympian strength. I winced. He seemed pleased.

"The beers are paid for," I said, "have another."

"Thanks. I will." He seemed pleased.

"Keep the change," I said to the barkeeper, heading out. She seemed pleased.

13

My week of Bomber's grace was flying by. To save time, I made a bunch of calls. First I called Ursula, Easy's second wife.

"Insurance," I said.

"Oh, that," she said. "I'd forgotten about that."

"He wanted to insure you?"

"Yes."

"For a million?"

"Uh huh."

"Did you do it?"

"No," she said. "I didn't like the implications. Easy said it was just a safeguard. If anything happened to me he would be just devastated. The million would make it easier."

"Did you buy that?"

"I wanted to, of course. We believe what we want to believe. But finally, I couldn't."

"What happened?"

"Easy was out of sorts—surly. Snide. He insisted I didn't trust him. I argued. I said I was superstitious about large insurance policies, like it could be a self-fulfilling prophesy. Understand, I was *crazy* about him. I couldn't believe my good fortune in attracting such a hunk. So I made a deal."

"What kind of deal?"

"I told him I'd give him the million up front. Then I wouldn't have an irrational fear I was worth more dead than alive. See, deep down I didn't have the self-esteem to believe this gorgeous specimen of manhood would want me for myself."

"Did he go for it?"

"Oh, he made a big show of rejecting the idea. Said he'd never take money from the woman he loved. He was old fashioned, he said. Rather die. That was the thing about Easy. He could sling it."

"So he didn't take it?"

"Finally, after much begging, he allowed as how he just couldn't take a gift like that, but if I insisted, he'd invest it for me. Sign me up for the Easy payment plan, so to speak."

"Do you know who his insurance agent was then?"

"Oh, no, I never interfered with his business."

I thanked her and hung up.

The company name on Easy and Melissa's insurance policy was Lloyd's of London. I called the number and was directed to a chap named Rory Dower. He had a British accent and a British reserve. It was only the gentle suggestion of a subpoena to haul his bones the two hours each way to Angelton that induced him to loosen up.

"I'm just the agent," he said. "I don't write the policies. But I remember this one—very tightly written as I recall. We know Mister Noggle's history, of course. We tend to be skeptics in this business—it's iron clad. No murders, no suicides, and we got very healthy premiums."

"Why would Easy go for this?" I asked. "There must be a catch."

"Well, again, to establish murder, you have to get a conviction in court. Perhaps he thought he had a foolproof scheme to kill his wife. Maybe he thought so, but Lloyd's doesn't just roll over and play dead."

"You'd investigate?"

"You bet."

"Did you this time?"

"Didn't have to. They have the culprit, who happens to be the beneficiary, in jail. They took care of it for us."

"What if she's acquitted?"

"She won't be, don't worry."

"What if the verdict is justifiable homicide?"

"It's still homicide. No cigar."

So much for the happy news from Lloyd's of London. Did Melissa know this? I expect she did.

Three seconds after I hung up the phone, it rang. It was Joan.

"How's it going, handsome?" she asked and my heart shot through the roof.

"So good now that I'm talking to you. You?"

"Likewise. Writing any music?"

"Not since you left."

"Don't you usually compose a piece for the case you're working on?"

"Yes, I do, but we're not really *on* this case yet. I mean, I'm just exploring the background. Bomber doesn't really want to take the case."

"Write something anyway. Piano and violin would be nice."

"Okay," I said. We talked on, making the phone company very happy, and as soon as we hung up I went to the piano and started doodling.

And I felt better.

Next morning I called the Bank of Angelton's lending department and spoke to a loan officer named George Sharpe.

"How's it going?" he said as though he knew who I was.

"Fine," I said. "I was looking for some info on a loan you hold on the late Fred Noggle's place."

We went over the Byzantine mortgage structure with its first, second and third loans.

"Not legal," he said.

He hadn't heard of Cornwell Securities, the name of the entity on the third trust deed but he told me some of those marginal lenders were over on Cornwell Street—as the name implied.

14

I parked near the taco place on Cornwell Street and moseyed up and down the sidewalks looking for something likely. On my first pass, I didn't see anything I thought a possibility. There was a curio shop, a small market, a store specializing in decorator hardware, another in plumbing supplies. On the corner, a Jiffy Lube. Saying the neighborhood was 'mixed' was brushing it with flattery.

Like a search party starting in the center and circling out, I widened my search area. A fast food sandwich place, a medical clinic, a butcher shop, a veterinarian, and there it was—staring me in the face—a two story old brick building that looked as if it could have stood on the corner of one of those old mining towns now morphed into a ski resort.

The windows weren't large plate glass storefronts like most of the neighborhood, but on one was sure enough painted in gold leaf:

Abogado

Another window, in more modest type, proclaimed the establishment's willingness to do business in the field of:

Bail Bonds

In a third window:

Español—and as an afterthought—*English*

The inside of the building was predictably dark. Not only were the windows small, they were covered by drawn shades. The law office was on one side of the entry, the bail bond operation on the other. There was a stairway leading to the second floor, but there was no indication of what rewards might be in store there.

I opened the half-smoked glass door to the Abogado and came face to face with a secretary who looked more like a sentry on loan from the Addams Family.

"Yes?" she said.

"Yes," I said. It seemed an appropriate response to the question. "I'm told I might find here a principal or two of Cornwell Securities."

"Well," she said in a huff, "I'm sure I don't know what you're talking about. This is a law office."

"And might one assume you have a broad spectrum of clientele?"

"We have many clients—"

"And you don't limit your practice to bail bonds?"

"That's another entity entirely," she said, letting her superior airs get the best of her.

"What's upstairs?" I asked, the soul of innocence.

"That's private," she said.

"Cornwell Securities private?"

"None of your beeswax," she said, expressing her sentiments with a touch of color.

I liked the way she was so protective of privacy around there. It bespoke they had something to hide.

"May I see the abogado?" I said.

"He's busy. I can make an appointment for you if you'd like." She paged through a book so seriously I expected her to offer me a Tuesday two years hence. I looked around the waiting room. Empty. I looked at another hammered smoke glass door with 'Attorney Foster Teague' painted neatly in the ubiquitous gold leaf. I heard no conversations behind the door. His busyness did not seem to involve another person.

"Who shall I say wants the appointment?"

"Tod Hanson," I said, "I'm Bomber Hanson's son."

While she was nonchalantly writing my name in her book and on a small appointment card, the door to Foster Teague's office burst open. The doorway was filled with an older chap—perhaps sixty—with a respectable belly draped in a Hawaiian shirt. He made no move to cross the threshold, but instead stared at me. "Bomber Hanson, you say?"

"Yes."

"What's his interest?"

"Doctor Melissa McHagarty," I said. "In jail for murdering her husband, Easy Noggle—a murder I have reason to think she didn't commit."

"Come in here," he said. It was not an invitation but an unhappy, yet necessary, command.

His office was gotten up like a frontier office in keeping with the old brick façade. His outer wall was the same brick, his desk was old time wood, as were his oak file cabinets. Overhead was a ceiling fan that turned lazily, almost creating some air movement.

He sat behind his desk. I sat facing him, though I couldn't be sure I saw any indication from him to do so.

He fixed me in his sights, and I thought he'd like nothing so much as to blow me out of there and never see me again. I just stared back—a pose that never brought out the best in me. But I didn't cave in.

"Okay, kid," he said, finally, fairly sneering, "I'm gonna save you some moves. I expect in time you could run us to ground, so okay, we got nothing to hide. What do you want to know?"

"Are you Cornwell Securities?"

"It's a bunch of investors; I'm the general partner."

"Meaning?"

"I take all the guff."

"Who are the other partners?"

He shook his head. "Doesn't matter," he said. "I'm the

69

general of record."

"You don't think I can find out who the partners are?"

"I expect with some extended legwork you can. You just won't get that from me. I speak for the partners. They'd all tell you to talk to me."

"So you loaned, was it, a million, to Easy Noggle?"

"About that," he said.

"Why?"

"He asked," he shrugged. "Needed more cash to complete his house."

"I understand your note carries an interest more than double the current rate."

"It's a third trust deed. We are way down the line for collection. Way more risk than a first. If we can't sell the house for what we appraised it, we could lose money, big time."

"But you'd have the house."

"And all the mortgage payments, back taxes, insurance. By the time we find a buyer willing to saddle himself with that white elephant we could be cleaned out."

"Guess the doc's in no position to make the payments where she is."

"Not hardly."

"What about the drugs?"

"Drugs? What are you talking about?"

"Doctor McHagarty says Easy pressured her to deal drugs. You know, make bucks for you."

"Me? Not for me—I don't do drugs."

"So you could sell them."

"Ridiculous! Never. We're lenders, not drug dealers."

I looked around at the shabby office. He sounded convincing, but the place didn't look any more like a lender's office than my broom closet cum office.

"So what do you say to the accusation that you wasted Easy because he didn't pay up?"

He shook his head in a gesture between sadness and disgust.

"Here's how it works. We loan money on houses. We take notes with the house as collateral. You don't pay, we take the house. We don't shoot you, that would be crazy. Dead men don't pay up."

"Why does the widow suspect you?"

He exploded with a short, terrifying laugh. "In her fix I'd be fingering anybody I could think of."

"So you're just your friendly corner lender taking big risks, lending at double the interest and hoping for the best."

"You watch too many mafia movies. We're lenders, not a crime family. I don't even know any Italians. The closest I ever got to an Italian is I had a Ferrari once. The thing never worked."

"Yeah," I said, counting my blessings I'd gotten as much out of him as I had. "Well, thanks for your help." As I got up to leave, I decided to spring on him the mystery name—the only name among Easy's collection of papers that I couldn't connect to anything: "The name Igor Sulwip mean anything to you?"

He looked blank, but I detected just a flicker of embarrassed recognition there.

"Never heard of him," he said.

But I knew he had.

Outside, on a hunch, I checked the small parking lot out back. The car I had seen at Easy's was in the handicapped spot—without a handicapped permit.

15

Bomber hadn't called me in—nothing so direct. He had Bonnie do it. Insult to injury in my book. The gorgeous airhead greeted me on my entry in the morning with, "Hiya, Sweet Meat. Your week is up." Her eyelashes accompanying to the tune of *Twinkle Twinkle Little Star* in all of Mozart's twelve variations.

So my first thought is, week's up, so what? Does that mean I'm obliged to go running into his rogue's gallery first thing? No, I thought, it does not. If I ignore it, maybe it will blow over. If he doesn't want to take the case anyway, why should I care?

I headed for my office.

I heard Bonnie Doone say to my back, "Need a hearing aid, Buster?"

Not a bad idea, I thought, then I could turn it off around Bonnie V. Doone. But I got the picture. It did not bode well for my plan. "Yes, yes," I said, "I hear you." But I proceeded into my closet/office and risked terminal claustrophobia by closing the door.

There was a note on my desk, put there while I was out by the incomparable Bonnie Doone:

> *From*: Sgt. Avery Knapp
> *To*: Lover Boy
> The vehicle in question is registered to Igor Sulwip at 798 Cornwell St., Angelton.

That was the address of Cornwell Securities and of Attorney Foster Teague.

I sat down at my desk, put my head in my hands and tried to force a solution to my predicament.

A great deal was riding on Bomber's mood. In some moods, admittedly rare, I could envision him picking up on my hints and embracing them as his own ideas.

On the other hand, sometimes I saw Bomber as the toughest nut in the universe with an uncrackable shell. Other times I thought, but couldn't be certain, I detected a marshmallow core. He was certainly not without feelings of humanity, it was just that most of the time I couldn't detect them.

I racked my brain for a plan, but my brain wasn't racking. Suddenly, I had this fantastic idea that I thought would give me the best shot at his acquiescence, if not his wholehearted enthusiasm. I had this inspiration that was all tied up in the reason I stutter with Bomber in the first place.

My thoughts were interrupted by a knock on the door and an off-tune stab at the *Indian Love Call* by the resident ingénue of Albert Avenue.

"He is calling youuu, ooo, ooo ooo ooo."

Ignoring Bomber was out of the question, unless I decided to seek gainful employment elsewhere. In the skateboard factory, perhaps, or possibly renting bicycles on the beach to tourists. I guess I had to face it. I was starting to *like* my job. Sure I'd still rather be writing music all day, if I could find someone to pay me for it.

I opened my door to find BVD still cooing, "You ooo ooo…."

"Thanks for the rendition, Maria Callas."

"Who's that?"

"Country Western star—before your time," I said. She didn't know the difference.

Bomber greeted me in his inner sanctuary with a hale and hearty, "Well, well, the prodigal returns." Then he frowned. "Bonnie tells me you sought to avoid our meeting." He shook his head and clucked his tongue.

"Bonnie's a t-tattle-t-tale."

"Sit, sit. *Sit!*" he said impatiently.

There on the hot seat in Bomber's rogue's gallery, I was stared at by not only Bomber but by all the luminaries from the four walls.

Intimidation.

I was in the untenable position of making a sale to a man whose mind was closed against buying.

"Well, what have you got to say for yourself?"

"Not much," I said, glum at what I thought of as wanting persuasive skills.

"So let's hear it. How did you spend the week I just paid for?"

If I had been hoping for any generosity of spirit in the matter from the great man, I was no longer. But maybe I'd get lucky, and lightning would strike one of us.

I began my narration of my week of investigation. With every disclosure I sought to impart a hint of the parallels I saw between Dr. McHagarty and my late sister.

I didn't see the slightest sign that Bomber was grasping it.

Though I thought I'd never get there, the end of my recitation came. I took out a handkerchief and wiped my chin. Bomber peered at me. Did he grasp something after all?

"So what's your conclusion? Did you find even a shred of evidence she didn't do it?"

I shook my head.

He held out his hands as though that ended it.

"Sometimes people do bad things because they can't do anything else," I said.

He looked at me quizzically for a long moment.

"Justifiable?"

"Sad, but m-maybe we have to ac-accept it."

I could only hope Bomber was thinking as I was. When Sis drove off the end of the pier, she did it because she couldn't do anything else. When Bomber went to pieces over it, it was because he couldn't do anything else. And when I—just a kid, really—stepped in and took over for my father—big, strong, infallible father—it was because in spite of my grief and social shyness, *I* couldn't do anything else.

"You think it was justifiable?" he prodded.

"At least," I said.

"Hm," he said, "hmm," and just sat there for enough time to relive the whole Sis episode.

"What do you want me to do?" he asked at last.

There it was. My opportunity—if I only had the guts. It was what they call a defining moment, but who was doing the defining?

"Does Melissa McHagarty r-r-remind you of anyone?"

His eyes did the dance of discovery. "No...I...should she?"

I nodded.

He frowned. "Who?"

"Someone c-c-close t-t-to uh-uh-us."

Was his subsequent frown genuine, or was he simply avoiding the obvious?

"Someone who d-d-did s-s-something s-s-so tr-tr-tr-tragic that was over in s-s-seconds. Never to b-be r-re-t-trac-ted."

His eyes were signaling more cognition, but he showed no sign of acknowledging the obvious. "So—this...person we know, did something like this—murdered someone—because she couldn't *help* it?"

"In a w-way."

His face was still fuzzy. He wasn't grasping it, I thought. But God knows I have been wrong before about what goes on in that head of Bomber's.

It was bull-by-the-horns time.

"A relative," I muttered, relatively free of stutter.

The news hit him between the eyes like a hot poker. His mouth dropped open, then snapped shut just as quickly. "You mean…?" he couldn't complete the thought. I thought if he tried *he* would start stuttering.

So I nodded, fighting to keep my eyes on his. His were not on mine.

"Couldn't do…anything…else," he said, and his eyes pinched shut to cut out the vision.

Was he wondering if I could really equate a suicide by driving a car off the pier in the middle of the night with murdering your husband? I thought so. He began, "Do you really…?" but stopped that thought in the bud.

We sat in a long, mutually embarrassing, silence. Believe it or not, I thought his discomfort greater than mine, but any revelation I'd hoped from him didn't materialize, and he dismissed me with a curt, "Let me think about it."

"Okay," I said, rising with a serenity that ended the day I saw Melissa McHagarty in court at her preliminary hearing. It didn't matter to me at that moment what Bomber thought. I had been able, however feebly, to make my case, and that was enough for me.

16

Before I knew it, Bomber showed up at my office door. "Let's go," he said.

I didn't even ask him where. I knew where. I wasn't sure why.

We climbed into the red Bentley for the jaunt to the lockup near the sewer treatment plant. Bomber liked to be seen in the Bentley—it was a validation of his success. If he ever advertised I thought he'd have a picture of himself leaning on the hood of his Chinese-red Bentley. The caption might be something like:

When you can afford the best...

I always sensed a vague discomfort in Bomber whenever he had to visit "the tombs," as he liked to call the jail when that mood struck him.

Visiting a woman in "the tombs" caused him the most uneasy feeling.

I was never sure of the source of his feelings. Was it because he felt himself too important a man to be slumming in this debased venue? (Modesty, it must be admitted, was not one of Bomber's more admirable traits.) Or did he have some slight sympathy for the unfortunate citizen who found himself so disadvantaged?

Melissa was already sitting in the visitor room when Bomber and I entered. I wasn't sure how Bomber brought this off. I suspected he had a contact who watched the parking lot and hustled her into the room so Bomber would not have to wait.

On seeing the door open, Melissa jumped up so violently the guard started toward her and put his hand on her shoulder and gently pushed her to her seat.

"Oh, Bomber, I'm so relieved you came."

"Your relief may be premature," he said, and she sank back at the blow, then brightened.

"For me," she said, "it is a big boost to my spirits just to be in the same room as you."

"Well," he grumbled, "you may thank my son for that."

She looked at me with liquid gratitude in her eyes, and mouthed a thank you. She turned back to Bomber. "You'll take my case?" she asked with becoming shyness.

Bomber ignored the question. "Tod has done yeoman's service investigating your case, Miss McHagarty." Melissa looked startled at Bomber's chosen form of address, but said nothing. I knew Bomber was in his courtroom mode, and when he wanted to bring the high and mighty down to the masses he diminished their stature with his form of address. Had he been on the other side, he would call her doctor this and doctor that until the cows came home. "I'm sorry to report he has not found one scintilla of evidence to support what I heard is your contention of innocence." He stopped dead with that and the respective looks on their faces were music incarnate—a slap on the bass drum by Bomber and a descending, yea sinking, glissando on a violin for her part of the composition.

If by Bomber's rather antisocial stare he hoped she would jump up and confess, he must have been mightily disappointed.

"Do you think Tod might have overlooked something?" he asked. "Are you holding anything back that might exonerate you?"

"I didn't do it," she said, like a zombie.

Bomber nodded his likely-story nod. "The evidence, alas, is otherwise. You admit to finding the body, to obtaining the syringe and the poison. And I understand your contention is you wanted to kill him, but didn't, is that correct?"

"Correct," she said. If Bomber could play courtroom, so could she.

"And why exactly *didn't* you do it?"

"Someone beat me to it."

Bomber nodded. "Who? And how? Your fingerprints were on the syringe."

"Easy had enemies."

"Don't we all?" Bomber said. "You think you were framed?"

"Perhaps."

"Why?"

"If I had done it, would I have left the syringe on the table?"

"An excellent point. But apparently you did," Bomber said. "Can you think of anyone he might remotely let in the house while he sat still for an injection? Even if they told him it was vitamin B12?"

"Maybe a girlfriend," she muttered.

"He *had* girlfriends, did he?" Bomber asked as though I hadn't told him all about them.

"I heard," she said without commitment.

"All right," Bomber said. "Here is what Tod found and what I deduce from it." He narrated flawlessly our conversation of my investigation. When he got to the insurance policies, he said, "Why did you agree to these policies? You knew he had some financial difficulty."

She barely nodded. Bomber was taking his toll, and she wasn't holding up that well. "Easy wanted it. I didn't care. I had no suspicions," she paused. "Oh, I see," she said. "You think *I* killed him for the money." She shook her head.

"And the clause saying no payoff if either implicated in the death of the other," Bomber prodded.

The doctor looked very sad at that moment. I couldn't decide if it was sadness brought on by innocence or guilt.

"I hope you don't think with my life at stake I'm thinking about money," she said.

"My dear young woman," Bomber said, "from time immemorial the rich and the poor, the educated and the stupid, have held money in the forefront of their thoughts, desires and ambitions, and that includes all those clerics who have taken vows of poverty. The only people who don't think about money are in the graveyard. The bulwark of our legal system—our courts—are set up to settle disputes about money. Some think the main function of the civil courts is the redistribution of wealth. You know the old adage—when people say: it's not the money it's the principle of the thing, it's the money."

I expected Dr. McHagarty to call Bomber an old cynic, but she didn't say anything.

"So don't tell me you're not thinking about the money. You can't surmount human nature, even if you are on trial for your life—perhaps *especially* if you're on trial for your life."

The doctor looked Bomber in the eye and said, "What do you want from me?"

"I don't want anything. I was told *you* wanted *me* to defend you," Bomber said. "But you have given me little to defend."

"I didn't do it," she said, with still less conviction. Maybe she was no longer sure, like a suspect worn down by merciless police questioning.

"Here's what I can offer you," Bomber said, and Melissa was jolted with encouragement. "Considering all the facts of the case, you might be able to cop a plea to attempted homicide, though it's a bit of a stretch. Another option is for you to plead justifiable homicide. I'm not keen on this kind of defense—turning the focus on the rotten victim, because no matter how rotten the victim—murder is *more* rotten. You could make a case that any murder of a husband by a wife is justifiable. It's just such a shady defense. Distasteful," he said. "I only wish the evidence were stronger. I mean, we can make him look like a mean sucker all right, but the question will always be, with you being such an intelligent, accomplished woman and all, why didn't you just walk out—leave him?"

"I didn't do it," she said like a broken record.

"If you come to terms with it," Bomber said, "I can try to work up a justifiable homicide case. He did have a first wife who I suspect he killed for a million dollar insurance payoff. His second wife gave him a million instead of signing any policy. He was possibly, yea likely, thinking of you next. If that's all he wanted in a wife, you may ask, why did he need a doctor? Prestige? Why were the policies necessary in the first place? You didn't need a policy on him, but that way he has a shot at convincing you it's all above board. Why insure you alone unless he has murder in his heart? Now *you* are in a position to collect, if you are not convicted of his murder. Anyway, I'm willing to try to work up a case with your permission—a case of justifiable homicide." He looked at her closely. "Of course you'd have to do without the insurance payoff."

McHagarty stared at Bomber as though he were crazy. "But I didn't *do* it," she said.

Bomber nodded the so-you-say nod and stood up. He uncharacteristically stuck out his hand to shake hers. "My very best wishes to you, Doctor," he said.

She held onto his hand and looked into his eyes, pleading, "Help me! Please help me!"

Bomber pulled his hand away. "I've offered the only way I know to save you. Taking your case the way I offered constitutes a compromise of my better judgment. The district attorney will plead, and rightly so, that if we let the citizenry decide murder cases on the basis of the victim's character there will be no tomorrow, and rightly so. Understand, I am not saying justifiable homicide will be an easy win. It might prove impossible with the evidence at hand. I am only saying it is your *only* hope—and I don't take hopeless cases. Good day."

We walked in silence to the car. I was grateful to him for giving her his time, but I couldn't express it.

Like Sis, Melissa was trapped in a cage not of her own making. Circumstances of life brought them both to a point where they were helpless.

In the car I said, "What do you think w-will b-become of her?"

"She'll go to trial and be convicted. I expect the sentence may be lightened somewhat, but she won't collect on the insurance."

"You think money's her m-motive?"

"I do."

"If she changes h-her m-mind and says 'f-forget the insurance, I'll g-go with the justifiable case,' what w-would you do?"

Bomber tightened his lips and squeezed one eye shut.

"I don't know," he said. "I'm not sure she could convince me or the jury."

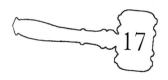

17

Dr. McHagarty stuck to her guns right up to her trial. Then she got cold feet and asked for Bomber.

"My terms?" he said to her on the phone.

"Your terms."

The judge allowed a recess in the jury selection process. Bomber asked the judge to have a heart. He was just coming on the case. Another month would be the minimum for his preparation. District Attorney Grainger screamed bloody murder. Seemed to think it was a Bomber-inspired trick of some sort.

The judge seemed to be okay with Bomber, but no judge likes his courtroom mocked by an attorney. So Bomber knew he had to walk a fine line, and he began his early supplications like any good penitent seeking a dose of religion—the forgiving kind.

When we got back to the office I was dispatched to the district attorney's office to pick up his witness list.

I cooled my heels in the D.A.'s waiting room for just over an hour before I caught sight of Webster A. Grainger III. He waved at me sheepishly and ducked back into his office.

I thought of barging into his office and demanding attention, but that wasn't my style. Instead I went to the secretary's desk and asked, "Do you know anything about the witness list in the McHagarty case?"

"He's working on it," she said.

"Working?" I expressed my surprise with my eyebrows. "Didn't he have it for the previous defense? The one we took over from?"

She smiled. "That was a different attorney," she said.

It was always so flattering to get special treatment from the D.A., but Bomber seldom got that kind of special treatment. Instead, *I* was getting the treatment.

"Look," I said, "I'm a patient man, but I have waited over an hour for something I have reason to believe was already prepared and given to the other attorney. Would Mr. Grainger like me to get it from the other attorney and have Bomber tell the judge what happened? Why don't you just give me the list before it is abridged for Bomber's eyes."

"Oh, I don't think Mr. Grainger would approve of that."

"Why don't you ask him?"

"He's working on it," she stonewalled again.

"So you said," I said. "Well, how about calling Bomber when it's ready. I don't mind wasting time, but Bomber has this thing about me earning my salary, meager as it is."

She smiled. "I understand."

"We'll look forward to hearing from you," and I turned to walk out just as the door to the district attorney of Weller County's door sprung open, and the D.A. himself smiled and thrust the witness list in my hand.

"Here it is," he said. "Took a little longer. I know Bomber is a stickler for these things. Just had to be sure it was ship shape."

I glanced at the list. There among the usual suspects— the cops, coroner, the experts on poison—was a shocker.

"Igor Sulwip?" I said, aghast. "No phone number?"

"He can't be reached by phone."

"Why not?"

"He's a guest of the county," he said, with a smirk.

"What's he going to testify to?"

"Oh," he said, trying without success to be casual, "just that McHagarty tried to hire him to kill her husband."

His smirk broadened into a world class smile. "Good luck," he added and ducked into his office, closing his door with great authority.

"Talk to him!" Bomber commanded when he heard my news from the D.A. about Fingers Sulwip being on the witness list. "Put the fear of God into him." That meant intimating that Bomber would crucify him on the stand, which he might very well do, and of course it never hurt to plant the seed that it might happen. Bomber loved to see witnesses tremble as he approached them for cross-examination.

I hot-footed it out to the slammer, where Fingers Sulwip did not look as I expected him to. He had the fingers all right—long, narrow, bony with arthritic bumps at the joints, but he was missing the bulbous nose with the road map of veins that you associate with the hardened criminal.

Sulwip looked rather benign, thin and nervous—the perfect foil for Bomber's courtroom antics.

We sat facing each other in the jailhouse visiting room—a banged up table between us. I could just see a series of cons kicking and pounding the table to protest the indignity of their arrest.

"See your name on the McHagarty witness list," I said casually without adding the implied, 'what else is new?' "Why in the world is a man of your stature slumming by doing the D.A.'s bidding?"

He didn't answer right away. I know he had discussed his options with District Attorney Grainger, and he seemed to be weighing them.

"So what's your connection to Doctor McHagarty?"

He shrugged his bony shoulders, as if to say, 'ah, why not?'

I'm sure Web Grainger told him what he could say and what he couldn't. Web knew Bomber could petition the court for this information, and though Web found it in his interest to obfuscate now and then, he knew some battles were not worth it. This was apparently one of them. And who knows, he might have thought the information would intimidate us, though I do suspect he knew better.

"She tried to hire me for a hit on her husband—Easy."

"And she didn't succeed?"

"Course not. I don't do that kind of work."

"Course not. What kind of work *do* you do?"

"Odd jobs."

"Such as?"

He shrugged. "Some construction—gofer work here and there."

"That's why you're here? Gofer work?"

"Nah. Mistake—misunderstanding."

"Uh huh. What sort of misunderstanding?"

"I don't have to answer any of these questions," he said.

"That's true," I said—"but when you get to court it's a different matter. Can't hide there."

"I could take the fifth," he said with some indignation at what he may have perceived as my obtuseness.

I nodded. "That would make you look real good—and it wouldn't bode well for the D.A. keeping his promise to go easy on you."

"I didn't say anything about that," he said with a worried look on his face.

"Well," I said, trying to get the message across that I wasn't born yesterday. "You didn't have to. Here, you sit at the pleasure of the county and you turn up on a witness list. No prisoner snitches out of altruism."

"I'm not a snitch," he insisted.

I nodded. "Circumstances," I said, waving around the room, "seem to indicate otherwise."

"Misunderstanding," he muttered.

"Yeah, well, you tell Bomber about that at the trial." I detected an involuntary tic at his eye. "Isn't going to be so easy," I said, "Bomber takes no prisoners."

Fingers licked his lips, but held his peace.

"So tell me, Fingers, what motivated you to turn down the commission to rid Angelton of one of its least desirable elements?"

"Told you."

"Tell me again."

"I don't do that kind of work."

"Would have been doing mankind a service."

Fingers looked at me with disgust. Bomber would turn that emotion to his advantage, but I didn't have that capability.

"So let's see if I have this straight. You're just a solid, upstanding citizen who is mooching on the county by mistake, who doesn't do the kind of work some of the other upstanding members of the community do. That is hits—wastes, bangs, murders, eliminates, kills—selected homo sapiens."

I was confusing him, but he didn't like the sound of it.

"Look," he said, "the D.A. tells me I don't have to talk to you."

"So why are you?"

His shoulders popped up. "Breaks the monotony."

"Well, you're in luck."

The sparse eyebrows above his blade nose bounced, then his eyes narrowed with suspicion. "Why?"

"When Bomber gets you on the witness chair, you'll be on a perpetual roller coaster. You won't be bored, I can guarantee you that. I thought you might want me to make it easier for you."

"How easier?"

"A free exchange of ideas," I said. "Give you a clue of what to expect from Bomber."

Fingers showed me what he thought of that by taking his bony, gnarled hand, placing it fingers up beneath his chin and flipping it out at me.

The moment of truth was at hand. Should I ask him about his car being at the house after the murder or not? I decided, finally, after staring at Fingers for a long moment, that it would be better strategy to let Bomber surprise him with that intelligence that he didn't know we had.

Fingers seemed relieved when I said goodbye—happy to be rid of me.

Bomber, on the other hand, was not happy with my news.

"Why didn't *she* tell us that?" he stormed in his egomaniacal lair in our Albert Street Victorian. "That's it. I'm withdrawing from the case. Notify Doctor McHagarty and the court immediately. I can't represent anyone who isn't up front with me—especially on a matter of such import."

"M-m-mayb-be he did it."

"What?" Bomber was startled. "Who did what?"

"M-maybe F-fingers did s-something with the syringe—p-put the poison in. D-did s-something so the doctor d-didn't have to t-tech-nically k-kill him."

He waved a hand at me. The hand of ultimate dismissal. "Academic, boy," he said. "I'm off the case. Let's turn our attention to those other clients who are honest and above board with us."

Bomber was boiling mad. He was in no mood to have me play devil's advocate. Every so often I get the feeling Bomber is experiencing a deference deficit. When that happens I have to be on my toes so I don't step on his.

I nodded silently and left the inner sanctum.

18

I knew I couldn't just let it go at that—not after all the agony I'd been through on the case. But I was beginning to let slip my high regard for Dr. McHagarty.

However, I decided I owed it to myself, if not to her, to find out why she had withheld this vital information.

I made an appointment to see her in jail.

When she was led into the visitors room, her face a combination of hope and vulnerability, my heart went out to her again. I thought if Joan ever left me for some guy whose lips pucker on a double reed instrument, I could do a lot worse than the doc.

I gave her a hint. "The name Igor 'Fingers' Sulwip, mean anything to you?"

I immediately saw the flicker of recognition on her face. "Oh, that turkey," she said. "He's the guy Easy hired to kill me." She shuddered, "I still can't imagine anyone doing that."

"Which part—the killing or the hiring?"

"Either."

"Hm," I said. "And that's all?"

"All?"

"How did you find out Easy hired Fingers to kill you?"

"One of my patients told me."

"How did he—or she—know?"

"Had some tenuous connection. A distant relative or something."

"What did you do about it?"

"I met Fingers with a witness."

"Who was the witness?"

"Oh, does that matter? I don't want to involve him in this mess."

"That's very noble, but with your life and liberty at stake, I'm not sure you have the luxury of protecting others."

"Well, it was Henry Ziggenfoos. He happened to be making a sales call. I was scared to death."

"You didn't think if he was hired to kill you he might kill Henry Ziggenfoos also?"

"I…I guess I wasn't thinking clearly. Anyway, we met at a lawyer's office. I thought that would be as safe as anything. I also alerted the police, and they were kind enough to send a car, which we could see outside the window."

"Clever," I said. "What was your conversation with Fingers? And was the lawyer present?"

"He was in his office. Fingers, Henry and I were in another room."

"What was the lawyer's name?"

"Foster Teague."

"On Cornwell?"

"You know him?"

"Yes."

"Well, he can verify it for you then."

"If he will."

"Yes—you're right. I never thought of that."

"Are you aware Foster Teague, and apparently some associates, loaned Easy a million on your house?"

"His house," she corrected me. "My name wasn't on the title."

"Did you know about the loan before Easy died?"

"Yes," she said. "He was being pressured to pay, and I was to buy these carloads of drugs to appease them."

"Who was pressuring Easy?"

"I don't know—Easy kept a lot of things from me."

"So what was your conversation with Fingers?"

"I was plenty nervous, I can tell you. I don't know if

anyone who hasn't experienced such a trauma as facing a man who is hired to kill you can imagine the feeling, the sheer terror. I mean, I must have been crazy to confront him—but what else could I do? Slink around, looking over my shoulder all the time? Trying to hide, while keeping alive by keeping my practice going?"

"Why did you confront him?"

"I thought if he saw me, he'd have compassion. Also, I thought if I outed him, he might not want to take the chance of being caught."

"So—what did you say to him?"

"Oh, I don't know. I was just so nervous. I think I said: 'I understand you've been hired to kill me,' or something."

"What did he say?"

"Oh, 'Who told you that?' or something."

"Did you tell him who?"

"No, I just asked him to deny it."

"Did he?"

"Of course."

"So then what?"

"I asked him how much he was being paid. He denied it again—so I asked what the going rate was. He said it depended."

"On what?"

"The ability to pay, the difficulty of the hit, the renown of the person."

"All of that making you an expensive target."

"Exactly! And I wondered where Easy was planning to get the money. I asked Fingers, hypothetically, of course, where a guy like Easy—down on his luck—would get the money to pay."

"What did he say?"

"The insurance policy."

"But didn't Fingers know the policy wouldn't pay off on a violent death?"

"Well, I'm sure Easy didn't enlighten him on that detail.

But I did. I'm not sure it registered with..." (Was she groping for the name or was it just too distasteful to pronounce again?) "Fingers."

"And so you left it at that?"

"Essentially. What else could I do?"

She didn't really expect an answer, but finally I couldn't resist. I said, "You could have offered to hire him yourself and turn the tables on Easy."

"Oh, yes," she said as though I had jogged a dim memory—"exactly."

"So you did it?"

"Did what?"

"Offered to hire him."

"Oh, not seriously. I was half joking to get more information. Like, when and where he was liable to do it."

"Well, I'm afraid I have some sobering news to break to you. Igor Fingers Sulwip is in jail, and he just happens to be on the D.A.'s witness list. You can bet the ranch he isn't going to say you were joking as he testifies *you* tried to hire him to kill Easy. And I wouldn't hold my breath expecting him to say *Easy* hired him first. I don't think that's in the cards."

I glanced at Melissa's eyes. They were absorbing the blow. "But what has he to lose telling the truth?"

"Lose, my dear? He has everything to lose. He has become a witness for the prosecution to shorten and possibly eliminate his jail time. There are, by the nature of the swindle, no written agreements. The D.A. can only recommend, he can't terminate a sentence. The judge may not agree with the D.A. Lot of pitfalls along the way—that's if it all goes perfectly according to plan. So it follows that if Fingers disappoints his savior, that old sentence will run its course and possibly more." I shook my head. "Hardest thing to break on the witness stand is a con who has the impetus of a reduced sentence at stake."

"Surely Bomber can make minced meat of him."

"Surely not. Oh, he can belittle him and his story— make him look foolish, even unbelievable, but you won't shake his story, and those that want to believe him will."

Dr. McHagarty frowned and dropped her head. "Doesn't look too good, I guess," she said. "I guess I messed up, didn't I?"

"I'm afraid Bomber thinks so."

"Bomber? You told him?"

"Told him? I *work* for him."

She nodded slowly, as though coming to a conclusion, but she didn't say anything.

So I did. "I'm afraid as a result of this memory lapse, Bomber has gone through the roof. He's talking about resigning from the case."

"What? You can't *let* him!"

"Oh, sometimes I wish I had that kind of power over him, but the fact is I'm so powerless in his presence I can't speak straight—I stutter."

"Don't let…" she began, as though she hadn't heard me, then abruptly stopped as though she had. "If he drops me, you have to do me a favor."

Uh oh, I thought, she's going to ask me step in. I know my limitations, in spite of the brief success I had in *She Died For Her Sins*. It was successful precisely because it was brief. I had no desire to tempt that fate again. I owed it to her to ask what favor she wanted.

"There is some more cyanide at my house. Bring it to me."

"Cyanide? Why?"

"I have rats in my cell," she said, and I almost believed her.

"Uh huh."

And she told me where it was.

19

When I got back to our Victorian house on Albert Avenue, I went directly to Bomber's office without stopping to collect my thoughts. They wouldn't have made much of a collection anyway. I decided to say whatever came to mind. I was through trying to protect and serve Dr. McHagarty. I'd believed her when she told the tale of Fingers Sulwip and her 'kidding' about a hit on Easy, but the more I thought about it, the stranger it seemed that a person of her intelligence didn't see fit to mention it to her lawyer.

My new insouciant attitude bolstered my confidence, and my knock at Bomber's door was, if I do say so myself, perfect.

I felt at home rather than intimidated sitting in the midst of the praising pictures on Bomber's wall. The heavy testimony to his greatness seemed to rest lighter on my shoulders. Unfortunately, it was not so light my stutter took flight.

I laid out her story in simple declarative sentences, without embellishment, flourish or persuasion, and Bomber seemed startled at my new demeanor in the case.

I ended my recitation with, "She was a fool not to t-tell you."

"Yesss…" he said slowly, as though not sure. "You say she wasn't *seriously* trying to hire him to kill Easy?"

"That's what *sh-she* says." I emphasized the she because I didn't want Bomber to think I bought it. But as I sat watching his face work over the proposition, I began to wonder if *he* wasn't buying it.

He sat, tapping a forefinger on his desk. "Give you any ideas, boy?" he asked, and the "boy" was inflected without its customary derision. And in that moment, with my father looking more like a father than an employer, I got the idea. I nodded and began to speak without my customary fear of being wrong.

"Self-defense," I uttered without the stutter.

He slammed his flat hand on the desk.

"Exactly."

I sat there stunned only a moment longer before Bomber jumped up and started for the door. "Come on," he said.

I stood. "Where are we going?"

"To the district attorney."

Without understanding, I followed. Bomber goes near the D.A.'s office only in cases of dire emergency.

I'll say this for our visit. Web didn't make Bomber wait like he'd made me wait.

Web looked at Bomber with a half-cocked eye. "Plea?" he said incredulously. "*You* want to cop a plea?"

"No, Sir, I'm not here to insult you. I'm here to bargain for an upstanding member of the professional community with a blemishless record and reputation."

Web waved a hand. "What's the offer?"

"Justifiable homicide. Self-defense."

Web shot Bomber a withering glance. That is, it would have withered anyone else besides Bomber. "That's not a plea. That's a copout. The last time I looked, justifiable homicide was not a punishable offense. Oh, so don't tell me, counselor, your offer is for me to capitulate to justifiable homicide and drop the case?"

Bomber said nothing. It was answer enough.

"So what am I missing here, Bomber? Easy, you say, wanted to kill her. So how is it he decides to take an injection from her—putting away his gun, or what have you, for the nonce? You think you can sell that to *any* jury as a clear and present danger?"

Bomber shook his head once. "Not important what I think. The important thing is what *you* think I can sell *any* jury."

"Well, you know better than that, Bomber."

"No, Mister Grainger, I was thinking more in line of perhaps third degree murder, and a respectable fine—say five thousand dollars and time served. She'd do probation as long as you wanted, I'm sure."

Web rolled his eyes. "I suppose I should thank you for this unprecedented offer, which I certainly knew you would not have made were not your position egregiously untenable, were not your client standing on the gallows with one foot on a banana peel—but fortunately for the state and the aggrieved citizens thereof, I am still in possession of my senses. Denied, counselor, denied, denied, denied."

We had barely cleared the door to the district attorney's office when Bomber let go of an explosive guffaw. "The old goat, he didn't have any idea I was pulling his chain."

"How s-so?" I asked.

"You don't think I couldn't have—*didn't*—write the script to his reaction before I flattered him with my presence in that hovel the good citizens of this county have bestowed on him—courtesy of my taxes," then he added as an afterthought passing his judgment on the insignificance of the matter, "and yours?"

Bomber was mightily pleased with himself—so much that I didn't dare get near his bubble with my pins. He shook his head and laughed out loud again once we were inside the Bentley. "Webster Arlington Grainger the third, he doesn't know what a great offer he passed up. It will only make my victory that much sweeter."

Well, I thought, optimism is surely a good thing, but over confidence isn't.

It was an intelligence I decided against sharing.

"Well, boy, get to work on the jury list. Show it to the doc. See if she knows any of them—patients or what have you. Tell her I've reconsidered only if she works herself into a lather over her fear Easy was bent on killing her—irreversibly so."

I nodded. No stutters in nods.

"What we want," Bomber continued, "is battered women, women abused as kids. Stay away from the machos who think the women folk are getting too uppity. I don't mind pansies," he said with his customary political incorrectness. "Anyone subject to violence—emotional or physical—our cup of tea."

Marching orders, he called them—the guy who got his name as a bombardier in the Korean war—only he never got to drop any bombs, thanks to the armistice.

And when I got marching orders from Bomber, I marched.

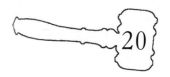

20

I took Melissa the jury list, and she marked three patients and the brother of a fellow book club member.

I asked her to make a list of people who might be stellar character witnesses for her, and she said she would.

She reminded me I had not gotten the cyanide from her kitchen.

I stopped at the office on my way to the mountain to get Bomber's slant on the poison. He authorized me to look, but not remove. I imagined him grandstanding in court with the information, for if we admitted Melissa killed Easy, where was the harm in pointing to the evidence? I suspected Melissa was still torn over admitting her guilt and I didn't want to believe it was the million buck insurance policy that was clouding her reason. I couldn't let go of the possibility that she really didn't intend to murder him, but that she was merely giving him what she thought was his vitamin shot, and someone else substituted the poison without her knowing it. Why else would she leave the syringe on the table?

It was a clear, sunny day with the sparkle of Angelton after the rain. It was a lovely, invigorating drive up to the house Easy briefly shared with Melissa. My thoughts drifted to Joan and the violin sonata I was supposed to be composing for her, but which I had not found time for. When I wound around the last turn that brought Easy's palatial mansion into view, I was shocked to see parked in the street Fingers Sulwip's car—the same one I had seen at the house on my first trip. But Fingers was in jail!

On the spur of the moment, I decided to park my car in front of the next house down the road, which was a good city block away. As I was walking back to Easy and Melissa's house, I heard a car engine revving up, and I saw the back of the car disappear around the bend without being able to identify the driver. I gave up the sudden notion of following him. By the time I got back to my car, he would have been long gone.

I used my codes (which I assumed the intruder also had) and let myself in the gate, and a good chunk of driveway later, the house.

I went right for the kitchen, where on a black granite counter I found the power strip Melissa had told me about. Into it were plugged a meat slicer, a Froth au Lait contraption for making foamy milk for coffee, a toaster and juicer. I couldn't understand why Easy didn't equip his kitchen with enough outlets to render the extension superfluous. Then I noticed in spite of all the appliances plugged into it, it wasn't plugged into anything. I took out my handkerchief and used it to turn the power strip over without leaving fingerprints. The back was screwed in, and I opened it with a pocket knife. There was nothing inside it.

Did I have the wrong thing? Or had someone gotten to it before me? Like my immediate predecessor on the scene?

I spent some time combing the kitchen for places this poison or other evidence could be concealed. No luck. I roamed the house again without seeing anything I thought was significant.

I went back to the room behind the bowling alley. As soon as I punched the code and opened the door I had the sense the room was not quite as before. I couldn't immediately put my finger on it, until my eyes traveled to the top of the desk.

There was a slip of plain tablet paper with a drawing of a pistol pointed at the head of a girl. Underneath it was written:

Fingers

and a phone number.

I dialed the number. There was no answer.

I drove back down the hill to the office on Cornwell Street where I had seen the same car—the one registered to Fingers Sulwip, parked in the lot behind the old-fashioned brick building. The car was there.

I went inside to the office of Foster Teague, attorney-at-law. I was not surprised to find him there. I was more surprised to find him willing to see me.

"I was up at Easy's house," I said, "and I saw your car parked there."

"Oh yeah? Why didn't you say hello?"

"May I ask what you were doing there?"

"Taking an inventory for a sheriff's sale. I've got to get what I can out of that turkey."

"The car you were driving?"

"What about it?"

"It is registered to Fingers Sulwip."

"Well," he said, showing a face of admiration, "you've done your homework."

"You're Fingers' lawyer?"

He shrugged. "He's my wife's sister's husband. What can you do?"

"And you drive his car?"

"I charge the battery for him every once in a while."

"Like today?"

"Like today."

"You also told me you never heard of Igor Sulwip."

"I did? When?"

"The last time we met."

"Maybe I misunderstood," he said.

"No," I said. "I'm quite sure you understood."

"Well," he said with dissembling hands floating at his sides, "I haven't been too keen on getting mixed up in this mess. We made Easy a loan—we're going to eat it; that should be enough suffering for that good deed."

There are many reasons for lying, I thought, and that one is no better or worse than the next.

"Does Mister Sulwip live here?"

"Here?" he seemed surprised. "No, why?"

"His car is registered to this address."

"Well, he did that without telling me. Fingers is, shall we say, not a man with strong roots. He moves frequently."

"In and out of jail?"

"It's happened."

"So you keep his car?"

"Sometimes."

"Fingers' wife?"

"She has her own car. They have a garage where they are now, but they live in it."

Oh brother, I thought. What next? I got back to the business at hand.

"May I see the inventory you made at Easy's house?"

He tapped his forehead. "It's in here," he said. "Large items—I'll be writing them down. You in the market for a large screen T.V., refrigerator, computer, a couple of cars that are probably leased?"

"Hardly," I said. "The T.V. is probably larger than my apartment."

"Yeah, well, keep working and save your money."

"Good advice," I said, not telling him there was nothing left to save from my meager salary.

"Happen to inventory Easy's hideaway?"

"Where's that?"

"The room behind the bowling alley."

"Didn't know about that," he said, and I couldn't tell if he was telling the truth. Then he added, cleverly, I thought, "Anything in there we can sell?"

"I don't know," I said. "I suppose that would depend on the buyer." I probed those rheumy eyes of his for a hint of something that wasn't there. "Anything in the...kitchen?" I asked.

He turned up his nose. "Nice refer," he said, and I was amused by the double entendre. Did he mean it? I couldn't tell. This was a guy who probably excelled at poker.

"The usual appliances—built-in stuff no good to me. You in the market for anything? I could give you first shot."

He did have a way with words.

I didn't want to get too fancy with Foster Teague. I always left the fancy footwork to Bomber. I bade Teague goodbye, and if I had half the poker face he did, he thought he had snowed me.

When I told Bomber the latest news, he sat back in his chair, fingers interlaced behind his head, his eyes on the special section of photos on the wall with presidents (I'm talking the U.S., not General Motors—though there was one of those somewhere).

I've been wrong before, but the great Bomber seemed to be warming to the case.

"Yes, yes," he said, "Teague and Fingers, not the most savory element by a long shot."

I nodded. How could I disagree?

Popping forward in his chair, his elevator shoes hitting the floor, "Me boy," Bomber said, "I have an idea. Wouldn't it be fun for you to solve this case for me? Here's what I'm thinking. You write down every scenario you can imagine, utilizing all the facts and suppositions at your command. Maybe seal 'em up in an envelope to be opened after the verdict—so you won't feel responsible for the outcome. Wouldn't that be fun?"

"Loads," I said.

"Huh?"

"Loads of f-fun," I said.

"Be good for you," he said. "Good training."

"Deadline?" I asked.

He waved a hand at me. "Oh, you decide. Sometime before the verdict." He was all smiles. "Of course you've got to get us a jury—that's got to be priority. But a man of your deep experience with jury scouting shouldn't blink at the task."

Left, right, left, right.

I marched.

The jury list, alas, was shockingly unfriendly. Too many

beer drinking macho guys, not enough battered women. I guess Angelton was not a community that lent itself to battered women.

Bomber was not happy with my report.

"Well," he said, "maybe we'll get lucky, draw the doc's patients and Web won't ask."

"Ha!"

"Any luck with that other project?"

"I'll g-get right t-to it," I said. I'm sure my speech halted a lot more than it would have, had he been a reasonable employer.

I padded back to my office. It was a fatal flaw in the architecture of our layout that I had to pass the centrally located airhead whenever I went between Bomber's and my offices. Fortunately for me, I didn't get a peep out of her, as her nose was buried in a movie magazine.

So what kind of scenario do we write? What actually happened or what does Bomber want to have happened? Or are they really the same?

Sure, someone else could have put the poison in the syringe, and Melissa could have injected it thinking it was the vitamin dose she put in originally. But Melissa denies giving him the injection. Now she'll have to admit it. I worried at her being able to keep her story straight. I was pretty sure Bomber would put her on the stand. He didn't have to, of course, but she was such a well-spoken, intelligent lamb—as far from anyone's picture of a murderess as you could get—and Bomber had to think that would help her case.

So did I write my scenario as though she were guilty or innocent? How angry would Bomber be if I crossed swords with him and made a case where someone else had done it?

That would be, as he said, fun.

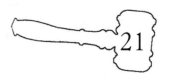

21

The time allotted us to prepare for the trial of the State of California versus Melissa McHagarty flew by. Now it was put up or shut up time.

I'd like to report that my investigation into the backgrounds of prospective jurors went well, even that it went okay, but it was a disaster.

The list was so unfavorable it seemed as though the district attorney had handpicked all the prospective jurors.

Predictably, Bomber was in a funk over my findings. "This case is a loser, and it is your fault I took it," he said. "I don't think I've ever felt I had a case this hopeless. Now on top of everything else we have a hanging jury."

"Can you get a c-continuance?"

"You kidding? We got one. No judge is going to give us another unless one of the principals dies or something. Web has got to be ecstatic about this jury. He'd see right through the motion and would oppose it with all he has." Bomber shook his head. "Delay is not in the cards, me boy. Who knows, the next jury panel might be worse. Maybe we'll get lucky and get one or two holdouts. But I don't see those in the cards either."

"I expect you'll m-make Melissa look h-heroic," I said.

"Yeah," Bomber said. "We make the victim the villain. Does that excuse the crime? I'm bound to tell you, I feel a lot more comfortable with an innocent for a client. Fingers Sulwip could be an unbeatable challenge," Bomber sighed a great load of air, then went on. "Guy kills his wife because she was a nag and he just couldn't stand it anymore. Justifiable?"

"No."

"Women get uppity now and then, you know. Justified?"

"No."

"These silly questions are just what the district attorney will ask, with the same answers and results. It's a loser."

"Not with y-y-you at the defense table."

Bomber beamed. "Well, I've always been partial to flattery," he said, "there's no gainsaying that. In this circumstance, rest assured, I shall have to fight to keep my head deflated. Well, me boy, let's look at them one-by-one in the hope some miracle will suggest itself."

I was very much afraid he was looking at me to suggest the miracle.

I'd put the prospective jurors in groups from *should be favorable* down to *don't touch with a ten foot pole—worth a peremptory*.

"Okay," Bomber said looking at the list and frowning through his mental calculations, "we have one hundred names here. There aren't twenty on this list Web will have to challenge. The judge will toss out Melissa's patients, that leaves what? Five or six we could call mildly favorable. They'll go like that," he said, snapping his fingers in front of his nose.

"Of course we'll challenge for cause, but the judge will never buy it. Prejudice, implied bias, actual bias. Maybe something good will show up." He shook his head. "Doesn't look good."

"S-sorry," I said as though it had been my fault.

"Say, you want to do me a big favor?"

"W-what?"

"Take the case."

"Oh...n-n-no."

"Your idea we stand up for the doc. You did a mighty fine job with the cop in that commie case."

I shook my head vigorously.

"No? Let me put it another way. You work for me—agreed?"

I nodded, I saw what was coming. A freight train at top speed with me tied to the tracks.

"And you take direction from me?"

I nodded.

"In other words, I'm the boss."

Nod.

"You're the employee."

Nod.

"And in good old-fashioned capitalist societies, employees faithfully take direction from their bosses—do what they are asked—or told?"

My nod was getting harder to execute and discern.

"So let's just say—for the sake of argument, you understand—that I ordered you to take the case."

I shook my head. "N-no!"

"On pain of dismissal?"

Boy, there was the question of my career. "We h-had a d-deal, d-didn't w-we? I w-was j-just g-g-going to d-do invest, investig-gation. I'm n-no g-good in c-court."

"So you'd quit before you took the case—after that aforementioned stellar performance?"

That case I wrote up in *She Died For Her Sins* was a one witness spur-of-the-moment fluke. There was no way.

"Yes! I'd q-quit."

"Interesting," he said. "Got a trust fund I don't know about?"

I shook my head.

"Oh," he said as though a light bulb had gone on in his head. "That new girlfriend is handsomely employed, isn't she? Well, I don't know how handsomely you can be employed playing the fiddle."

"M-more than t-twice what I make."

"Hmm, well, I suppose in this *modern* day, some young men are willing to live off the fruits of the labor of a female of the species. Can't imagine it myself, but they do say there is no accounting for taste."

Well, he had me going there. He knew my absolute terror of speaking in public. He knew that I'd fall on my face, and that could hardly make him look good. In retrospect (ah, lovely 20/20 hindsight), I realize he was pulling my chain—and I let him pull—held onto the chain for dear life and muttered something about being a waiter.

"Well, you'd be well qualified," he said.

No—he couldn't have been serious.

"Ah, give it a try, boy," he said, not giving up. "I'll help you every step of the way. Get your feet wet. A couple cases with me at your side..." he stopped. He must have remembered the stutter in his presence (when I knew he was there) "or back at the office—out in the hall—anywhere you want me."

It was my nature not to think about how valuable I was to him. I knew it, he knew it, and yet I let him bamboozle me. So badly I was actually considering my options, running the list of restaurants through my head. Did I want a high end with fewer tables and bigger tips or medium to low end where I'd run myself ragged but probably make more money?

But, I thought, get hold of yourself. We're two days from the trial. No way would he throw me to the wolves like that.

"That your final word?"

I nodded resolutely.

"So be it," he said.

"Sh-shall I l-look for a j-job?"

"Why?" he said startled. "You don't like this one?"

My face was red, but it held a large smile of relief.

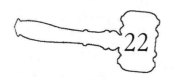

22

The media was outside the courthouse in force. Bomber graciously manipulated them on his way across the vast lawn to the courtroom.

"I'm proud to be associated with this wonderful client. Anybody who's had the good fortune to know Doctor McHagarty knows there's not a vindictive bone in her body."

"May we quote you?" a brave soul shouted out.

Bomber smiled. "Can't stop you," he said. "Of course, I wouldn't want to prejudice the jury."

We cleared the press and climbed the handful of steps to the huge, ornate Spanish courthouse. We trod across maroon colored Spanish tile to the oak door that led to the courtroom where our case was to be tried. There were people all over the hallway hoping to get a seat in the overfull room.

It was unusual to draw a crowd for jury selection, but such was the high profile of Bomber and the case. The community's regard for Dr. McHagarty was such that the 300 odd seats in the courtroom had filled as soon as the doors opened.

Bomber hadn't asked for a delay. "Don't want to start the thing off as a crybaby. Heads up, shoulders back. Let's take on the lions."

I followed Bomber down the aisle to the defense table. He waved and smiled like an underdog politician to anyone who looked familiar. This newfound gregariousness signaled to me just how hopeless he felt the case was.

We sat at the defense table. Bomber glared at the list of jurors in my seven categories, as though willing the list to improve. He turned to look at the prospective jurors as they came into the courtroom. Not a happy looking bunch of campers.

Of the 100 prospects for the jury, a good 23—almost two juries—had landed in the lowest category, *Don't touch with a ten foot pole.*

The second category, *Worth a peremptory,* had 27 names. That gave us 50 jurors to dispense with and only 20 peremptory challenges.

The grim statistics were staring Bomber in the face. He was staring back, but I noticed it wasn't changing any of the numbers.

"Maybe you were a little hard on some of those?" he asked without evidencing a lot of hope.

I knew I wasn't, but I shrugged to give him hope.

"Well," he said analyzing, "I take it you don't see anyone in this bunch who would go to the mat for us? Hold out for acquittal if eleven were for conviction?"

I shook my head.

He nodded shortly, "So be it," he said with a sigh. "So be it."

The district attorney, Webster Arlington Grainger III, came into the room surrounded by his retinue of assistants, fresh out of law school and eager to please. They spread Web's papers out on the desk, and it looked like they had done the same homework on the jury pool as I had. I wondered how different their view of the pool was from ours. Web and crew were followed by a sheriff's matron leading our client to our table. Bomber and I tried to look cheerful. We all smiled—sort of.

A few moments later Judge Hiram Pendegrast came in from behind the bench, solo.

Bomber leaned over to whisper, "Doesn't need any kids to prop him up, like Web."

Bomber had a nice range of whispers—one that could be heard only by me at his side, the one used for our prior conversation about the jury list, another to be heard by most of the courtroom—the one that got him in most trouble, which was the one he used now, to be heard by the prosecution. If it spilled over to be heard by the first few rows of the jury pool, so be it. The trick was keeping the judge from hearing it. Bomber didn't always succeed at that, but as long as the district attorney heard it, it drove him nuts.

With a few words of welcome from Judge Pendegrast, we were underway.

The judge looked lost in his robe. He was gray, but not an eminence. He reminded me of a career politician, who, at the end of his days, was rewarded for his faithful service with a judgeship.

My father leaned over to me again. "Was a district attorney," he whispered about the judge. "Tough on crime, tough on us." It reached my ears only.

Judge Pendegrast addressed the panel and asked if anyone knew any of the principals. And so we summarily lost our entire favorable pool.

Next he asked if serving would be a hardship for anyone, and we got the usual whiners with a wide range of excuses. Judge Pendegrast listened patiently to them all and didn't seem in a humor to be liberal about excusing them. The district attorney was not asking the death penalty, so that took an excuse from a number of them.

The judge finally excused 11 of the 96 remaining, leaving us with 85. If all 40 peremptories were used, we'd have 45 left, most of whom Bomber would be well advised to challenge for cause—if he could only find a cause that would fly with Judge Pendegrast.

We still thought, all things considered, we'd rather have women than men. The seating of the first twelve yielded two women. Both seemed to have trouble-free lives. One was a Republican Committee woman—tough on crime and bad for us. Esther Upshaw was Bomber's first target.

"Mrs. Upshaw, is it?" he asked, looking at her as though he wanted nothing so much as her friendship.

"Yes." She was a solid woman in her early fifties, who didn't show any signs of nonsense in her character.

"Active at all in politics?" Bomber asked her.

"I'm a Republican Committee woman."

"Ah, good. Have you any special feelings about trial lawyers?"

She smiled and squirmed a bit. "I think contingency fees and class action suits where lawyers make more than the clients might be getting out of hand."

Bomber smiled and nodded, as if to encourage her. "How do you mean, 'out of hand'?"

"I think juries often give huge outsized awards based on emotion."

"Do you know that I sometimes do that sort of work?"

"I may have read of a case or two," she said.

"And what did you think?"

"I don't remember."

"Think I may have gotten an unreasonable amount for my client?"

"I don't know that I thought about it."

The judge cut in. "Bomber, I'll try to save some time. Mrs. Upshaw, would whatever feelings you have for tort lawyers prejudice your thinking in this case?"

She shook her head. "I don't think so."

"Would you give any consideration at all to the fact that Mister Hanson is a tort lawyer and Mister Grainger is not?"

"No."

"And do you know the difference between a civil case, which is tried for monetary awards, and a criminal case, which is a matter of someone allegedly breaking the law?"

"Yes."

"You may pursue a different line, Mister Hanson."

Bomber was chagrined, but he was trying to play humble pie, at least in the beginning. So he nodded and said, "Thank you, Your Honor." But it was a presaging of what was to come—very little leeway for Bomber to obfuscate in juror selection. The little prejudices and biases that everyone had and denied were not to cut any ice with Judge Pendegrast.

Bomber easily went through his 20 peremptories, but near the end it got dicey—around numbers 19 and 20. The panel was bad enough stuffed to the gills with *Don't touch with a ten foot pole* and *Worth a peremptory*. There were still one or two that had not been called who we deemed worse than any already sitting.

Bomber took his chances and excused two from the worst group.

The next pair contained the all-time worst possibility—a guy we thought would not vote for us if hell froze over.

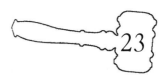

23

Then Bomber took a chance I'm not convinced was worth taking. I didn't challenge him on it because I knew he would say,
'When you try the cases, you make the decisions.' The twelfth
juror seated was the worst of the lot. A man with a history that
bespoke violence to women—not ideally poised to let a woman
free who had killed a man not as bad as he. But we were out of
peremptory challenges, and Bomber sought to show cause why
the juror shouldn't be seated. That was always a sensitive business. If you weren't careful, your zeal for your client would so
aggravate the juror who might feel he was being made a fool of
that he wouldn't vote for your side no matter how solid your
logic. For a man convinced against his will is of the same opinion still.

There were two hoped-for outcomes of the merciless
grilling. One was that the judge would dismiss for cause because
you had shown cause for dismissal, the other was that you had
alerted the prospect (as well as the other jurors) that you had
serious doubts about his objectivity. So he would bend over
backwards to be fair, rational and objective. And if he didn't, his
fellow jurors would remind him of his duty and his promise.

The juror's name was aptly Axel Johnson, for he looked
like a truck axle with a transmission for a belly, and greasy hair
and shoes. He looked at Bomber with a quiet, seething disdain,
before the first question passed the advocate's lips.

"What is your occupation, Mister Johnson?"

"Mechanic."

"What kind?"

"Autos, trucks."

"Have your own business?"

"Nah."

"Who do you work for?"

"The Edison Company."

"Keep their vehicles ship shape, do you?"

"Yeah."

"Would you like to serve on this jury?"

Axel shrugged. "Makes no never mind to me."

"Do your duty as a citizen?"

"I guess. Get off work, too," he got a laugh from the troops and was pleased with himself for it.

"Any violence toward women in your background, Mister Johnson?" Bomber got him back to earth in a hurry.

"Nah," but his eyes shifted all over the place.

"Married, are you, Mister Johnson?"

"Nope."

"Were you?"

"Once upon a time."

"That means yes, you have been married?"

"That means yes," he said with a tight mouth.

"Divorced?"

"Yeah."

"What caused the divorce?"

"I couldn't stand her." Another titter from the audience.

"That's too bad," Bomber said. "How did she feel about you?"

"The same, I reckon."

"Ever anything physical between you?"

"Well, sure, in the beginning, but she soon tired of that." More laughs. He was becoming a regular comedian.

Bomber played dumb. He nodded and paused until the troops simmered down. "Punch her out a little, did you?"

Axel Johnson shifted uncomfortably in his chair and his skin, "She may have got out of line a few times."

"Out of line? How so?"

114

"Don't remember specifically," he said, pursing his lips. "Lot of back talk. Just had to establish who was the boss around there."

"Ever have the feeling your wife might try to kill you?"

"She wouldn't dare."

"Ever think about it?"

"Not really."

"Does that mean you thought about it, but not much?"

"It means I didn't really think about it."

"Is not *really* thinking about it the same as never thinking about it at all?"

"Yeah, well, I guess. You know, it might have crossed my mind like those things do, but I certainly never thought she'd do anything like that."

"Certainly?"

"Yeah, that's what I said."

"May we approach the bench, Your Honor?"

"You may."

Web, Bomber and I went up to the Judge's bench. We were standing, he was sitting. Just another less-than-subtle example of the difference in our status.

"Your Honor," Bomber began, "in a jury pool hopelessly disposed to conviction of my defendant, we have finally drawn the worst specimen of macho chauvinism. 'Women get uppity'? 'Put them in their place'? Really, we're in the twenty-first century, but this man is a millennium behind us. I respectfully request you release him for cause."

Judge Pendegrast didn't reject the idea out of hand, which showed some objectivity. "Mister District Attorney?" he asked, turning to Web.

"I would just as respectfully oppose the motion. Perhaps there would be some small relevance if his wife had tried to kill him, but there's no evidence of that. He barely thought about the possibility. And he doesn't strike me as a man who sees his wife as Doctor McHagarty, or any kind of doctor at all. He's a mechanic."

Bomber returned to the fray: "I think this man was a chronic abuser. Easy Noggle was an abuser. I might be able to get the real story out of him, but at what price? I say let him go peacefully with his self-respect in tact."

The judge turned to the witness. "Mister Johnson, this is a case where a woman killed her husband. The defendant may claim it was self-defense because he was abusive. Do you think you can listen to the evidence presented and keep an open mind, and judge the defendant on the merits of the case, without any prejudice?"

"I guess so."

"Well," the judge said, giving us momentary hope, "don't guess. Yes or no? Can you be a fair and impartial judge of the facts presented in this courtroom or not?"

"Yeah," he said, "I can."

Why he wanted to be on a case when so many were looking for an out, I didn't know. Perhaps his statement about getting off work was it—probably a nagging co-worker—probably an uppity woman, but he got his place in the twelfth chair.

Judge Pendegrast wanted two alternates. One, praise the Lord, was a woman. There were only two women on the jury of twelve. This was a case that would certainly test Bomber's mettle.

The judge called a recess before we got down to business. Bomber was mighty glum.

We took Melissa into a conference room with a guard standing outside the door in case she bolted. Silly as the notion was, I thought with the makeup of the jury, bolting could well be her best option.

"Well, young lady," Bomber began when we were all seated around the table, "if I've had a tougher case, I don't remember it. I've had worse judges, but since he used to be a district attorney, he sees things from a prosecutor's perspective. I don't remember having a worse jury for our purposes. It is so bad I'm thinking we might be better off maintaining your innocence. Let's see what Web comes up with. Keep our counsel, so to speak, until it's our turn. I won't make an opening statement, so I won't have to tell them what our case is. That's in case we want to change it." Bomber looked her in the eye. "Still maintain you didn't kill Easy?"

"Yes," she said, looking back and giving as good as she got.

"Hmm," he said. "If only we had some plausible theory for an alternative. You still can't think of anyone?"

She shook her head. "I wish I could. Easy had a lot of enemies, I just can't make any of them fit the circumstances."

"Yeah," Bomber said, "well, okay. Here's what we might expect: Web will open with a statement about what he is going to prove. We'll have the police and the coroner, maybe a fingerprint expert, and the star will be Fingers Sulwip, who will tell his tale about you trying to hire him to kill your husband. He will conveniently leave out any mention of Easy hiring him for a similar mission, with you as a target. I'll try to break him of course, but cons who come to testify from the slammer seldom crack. It may be obvious they are lying, but they stick to their story. Unfortunately, we don't seem to have any witnesses that can or will corroborate our view of things."

Bomber leaned closer to her, "I trust no money changed hands between you and Sulwip? No down payment or anything?"

"No."

"What about this person who Tod found at your house?" He turned to me, "What's his name, Tod?"

"Foster T-Teague."

"Yeah—you know him?" he asked her.

"He made Easy the final loan to complete the house."

"Was he a friend?"

"He was just a loan broker…as far as I know."

"Any idea what he was doing snooping around your house?"

She shrugged her shoulders. "Maybe he was looking for hidden money or something to repay the loan."

"Okay. Now you haven't discussed this case with anyone, have you?"

"No."

"Don't. They'll probably set someone up in the slammer to get chummy with you. Don't respond to questions. If we change our approach we don't want anyone reminding us of different motives."

Time was up. We went back into the courtroom, Melissa accompanied by the sheriff.

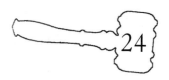

24

You could tell from the moment Webster A. Grainger III stood to make his opening statement, his confidence in his case was supreme. His smile, his courtly bows, all bespoke a man secure in his position.

If I had been trying the case, I would have been intimidated. Bomber didn't intimidate easily, but there was no gainsaying he was not exuding his usual *savoir faire*.

Web was so optimistic, he didn't dwell on the details of what he would prove, but merely ticked off the witnesses. "The police, the coroner, the fingerprint expert, the salesman who sold her the poison and the man she tried to hire to kill her husband.

"And then there's the insurance policy," the district attorney continued. "One million dollars to the doctor if her husband died. That will come into evidence in due course. We will demonstrate means, opportunity and motive. Those initials spell mom. As the testimony unfolds, remember: m-o-m. You won't find any theatrics on our side of the case. Everything we show will be represented by m-o-m, mom."

A little corny, I thought, but catchy.

Web called his first witness.

Avery Knapp, the policeman called to the scene of the crime, was sworn in with a sidelong glance at our table. On our last case with Avery Knapp as a witness for the prosecution Web made a fuss, and I was forced to substitute for Bomber. The consensus was it helped our case—sympathy for me and all that.

Web asked Avery Knapp all the foundation questions:

when did he get the call, when did he arrive, what did he find and what did he do with the evidence?

Avery was a pro, and he answered succinctly.

When Web said, "No more questions," and sat down, without saying, "Your witness," or even looking at us, I could feel Bomber chuckling beside me—"*Hn hn hn noh*," but he didn't move.

The judge looked down at him, "Any questions, Bomber?"

"Oh," Bomber seemed startled at the idea. "Sorry. I was waiting for Web's motion."

"What motion?" the judge showed confusion as he looked at Web, who merely shrugged.

"Do you have a motion, Mister Grainger?"

"No, Your Honor."

"Oh," Bomber said, "sorry. Last time we had Sergeant Knapp, Web felt it would be a conflict if I asked the questions, so the boy did it. I just thought…"

"Do you have any objections, Mister Grainger?"

"No, Your Honor."

"Very well. You may proceed, Mister Hanson."

Bomber grinned at Web who was trying to hold on to his composure, but not returning Bomber's stare.

"Now, Sergeant Knapp," Bomber asked, "who was at the scene of the crime when you arrived?"

"Doctor McHagarty."

"Anyone else?"

"No."

"Did you check the house to make sure there was no one else there?"

"No, I asked Doctor McHagarty. She said there was no one."

"So you took her word for it?"

"Yes."

"A large house is it?"

"Objection," said Grainger.

"Yes, sustained. Indefinite," the judge said.

"All right. Can you estimate how large the house was?" Bomber asked.

"Large," Avery said, and got a chuckle from the audience.

"Do you live in a house, Sergeant?"

"Apartment."

"What size?"

"One bedroom—maybe eight to nine hundred square feet."

"How many of your apartments would fit into Doctor McHagarty's house?"

He thought a moment. "Maybe ten or so."

"Could there have been someone squirreled away without your knowing it?"

"I suppose."

"Someone perhaps the doctor didn't want you to see?"

Avery Knapp shifted in the witness chair. He was clearly uncomfortable at the inference he might have been lackadaisical in his investigation.

"Possible," he admitted. "Though I heard nothing, and Doctor McHagarty told me…"

"Just so," Bomber said, "and you believed her?"

"Yes."

"Why?"

"Objection. Calls for conclusion."

"Well," Bomber said, "it's *his* belief."

"Overruled."

"I believed her because she is believable! A doctor—well known and respected—I didn't see any reason for her to lie about someone being there. Besides, I saw no evidence of another person, or persons."

"You were on which floor?"

"The upper floor."

"Which constituted what part of the house?"

"The living area—living room, dining room, kitchen and master bedroom—I believe."

"What was downstairs?"

"I didn't go downstairs."

"Did anyone from law enforcement, to your knowledge, go downstairs?"

"Yes, the lab boys."

"What were they looking for?"

"Clues of intruders or anything else that might be pertinent to the case."

"Did they tell you they found anything?"

"Nothing pertinent."

"Did they tell you about the bowling alley?"

"Objection. Assumes facts not in evidence," Web said.

"Well, okay," the judge said, "you may rephrase."

"Did they tell you what was downstairs?" Bomber asked.

"Yes."

"What did they tell you?"

Sergeant Knapp smiled broadly. "There was a bowling alley," he said. "A movie projection room, pool room, jacuzzi, and five bedrooms."

"No office?"

"No."

"No secret rooms?"

"Not that I know of."

"Sergeant Knapp, you said on direct examination you found a syringe on the dining room table?"

"Yes."

"Did you find the vial that had contained poison anywhere?"

"No, sir, I did not."

"Did anyone to your knowledge?"

"No, sir."

"All right, Sergeant. You spoke with Melissa McHagarty on the day of the crime?"

"Yes."

"What was her demeanor?"

"I'd say she was shocked."

"Did she seem like a woman who'd just killed her husband?"

"*Objection!*" Web was on his feet. "Calls for a conclusion. No foundation."

"Certainly a conclusion a man in his line of work can make."

The judge held up his hand. "Mister Hanson, please don't comment before I rule. The objection is sustained."

"I stand corrected," Bomber said, ducking his head in his patented bogus bow. He turned back to the witness.

"Sergeant Knapp, on direct examination, I believe you said you have been a police officer for over twenty years, is that correct?"

"Yes—twenty-three years."

"In that time, how many murder suspects have you questioned, approximately?"

"Oh, I'd guess somewhere in the neighborhood of seventy to eighty."

"Do you find yourself speculating on the guilt or innocence of the person you are questioning?"

"Yes, I do."

"And did you speculate in this case?"

"I did."

"What were your feelings at that time, concerning the guilt or innocence of Doctor McHagarty?"

"I thought she was innocent."

"Thank you, Sergeant. No further questions."

Web jumped up. "Sergeant Knapp, in your experience, have your hunches ever been wrong?"

"Oh, yes."

"Often?"

"I wouldn't say often."

"How often?"

"I don't know—ten percent, maybe a little more."

"And what was it about Melissa McHagarty that made you speculate on her guilt?"

Nicely put, Web, I thought.

The sergeant shrugged. "I don't know. She just didn't seem nervous. Answered all my questions without a lot of forethought. Was in a state of shock—surprise—she seemed surprised."

"Did you ask her if she'd killed her husband?"

"Yes, I did."

"And what did she say?"

"She said she didn't do it."

"Was she able to give you any names of suspects, anyone *else* who might have used her syringe and her poison?"

"Objection," Bomber said, "without foundation."

"Sustained."

"In your questioning," Web continued, "did you discuss the murder weapon?"

"We did."

"Did she recognize the weapon?"

"She did."

"What did she say about it?"

"That it was hers. She used it to give Easy vitamin and testosterone shots."

"Did you ask about the poison?"

"Objection."

"Sustained."

"To your knowledge, what was the cause of death?"

"Objection," Bomber said. "I'd rather hear that from the person who made the tests."

"Oh, all right, Bomber," Web said peevishly. "I was only trying to save time."

"My client could go to prison for a long time. Let's not worry about time now."

"Your Honor?"

"Yes, Mister Hanson, you *know* better than that."

"I stand corrected."

"All right," Web said, "I'll excuse this witness and call Coroner VanWert to the stand."

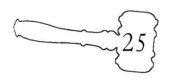

25

The coroner did his duty for Web. He spoke of the poison being potassium cyanide, a fast acting potion that shuts all the body systems down. At his inquest, Dr. McHagarty's then attorney had made no objections, asked no questions.

"Coroner," Bomber asked as his first question, "for my own information, did Doctor McHagarty ever confess to you, or to anyone in your hearing, that she had committed this crime?"

"No, she did not."

"Did you discover anything in your tests that indicated she, rather than anyone else, had committed this crime?"

"No, sir."

The fingerprint expert, Carlton Hennessey was next. Web led him through the rigmarole about fingerprints and how difficult it was to get a good set under most circumstances, but he did allow as how he had managed to get a portion of a right hand thumbprint of the defendant from the syringe.

It seemed to me Web had glossed over what could have been an important piece of evidence.

Bomber thought so. When it was his turn to question the expert, he began by submitting a blown up picture of the syringe as it was photographed on the dining room table at Easy's house after the crime.

"Now, Mister Hennessey, so the jury and the rest of us can get a perspective on our testimony for the prosecutor, I'm going to show you this picture of the syringe in question—the one you said had a thumbprint of the defendant on it—and ask you to point out exactly where that thumbprint was on the syringe. For simplicity we can say this part is the plunger (he pointed to the plunger), this part is the barrel, and this is the needle. Where was the print?"

"It was on the barrel, about one fourth of the way down from the plunger to the needle."

"About here?" Bomber asked, pointing to his estimation of the distance.

"Yes."

"Are you familiar with the operation of syringes?"

"Yes. Somewhat."

"All right, Mister Hennessey, when you use a syringe, how do you depress the plunger? With a finger…or a thumb?"

"Thumb."

"Using a finger to depress the plunger would be awkward, wouldn't it?"

"Yes."

"More difficult than using the thumb?"

"Yes."

"And yet the only print you found was on the barrel of the syringe?"

"Yes."

"And that was a *thumb?*"

"Yes."

"Did you find the defendant's thumbprint on the plunger?"

"No."

"Did you find other prints on the syringe anywhere?"

"We found nothing discernable."

"Does that mean someone else could have handled it? Say, with gloves?"

"Yes."

"Now, would you say fingerprinting today was more of an art or a science?"

"I think it's both."

"Can you explain that? Which aspect is science, which is art?"

"The lifting of the print from the respective surfaces is a science. Transferring the image to a plate for reproduction and viewing for comparison is science. The actual comparing of prints lifted at any particular venue with prints on file with the FBI tends to be more of an art."

"And the results of this comparing of prints by a human being are sometimes wrong?"

"They can be."

"Are they ever?"

"Yes."

"How do you account for the errors?"

"Objection," Web said. "He can't know—out of the scope of his knowledge."

The judge said, "He's asking for his accounting. He's an expert in the field. You qualified him as such. I'll overrule the objection."

"All right, Mister Hennessey, how would you account for the errors in comparing fingerprints?"

"Sometimes it's a matter of the quality of the print lifted—the clarity. Sometimes we get only partial prints, and that can be problematic. Sometimes the agent who is doing the comparing could be new and inexperienced and might make mistakes."

"I suppose even experienced agents can make mistakes."

"Wherever you have humans you can have mistakes," Hennessey shrugged. "But mistakes are rare," he added in defense of his profession.

"But they do happen?"

"Yes."

"Now, you spoke of partial prints. I take it that means part of a finger or thumbprint."

"Yes."

"And I suppose the smaller the part, the more chance of error in identifying the print?"

"Yes."

"What percentage was the defendant's print—her

thumb on the barrel of the syringe?"

"About thirty-five percent."

"Just a tad more than a third?"

"Yes."

"So would you say in that case, the chance of error was two out of three, or roughly sixty-six percent?"

"I couldn't estimate that."

"Might it be more than sixty-six percent if you only had thirty-five percent of a person's print?"

"Objection," Web said from his table. "He's already said he couldn't estimate."

"Just trying to clarify," Bomber said.

"I'll let him answer if he can," said the judge.

"Could it be more than a sixty-six percent chance of error?" Bomber asked.

Carlton Hennessey said, "I really couldn't say."

"In your experience, is there a correlation between the amount of the print you lift and the ability to make a positive identification?"

"Not to my knowledge."

"All right, but as an expert, you know mistakes are made?"

"Yes."

"And fingerprint identification is not totally an exact science."

"That's correct."

"Thank you, Mister Hennessey. No more questions."

Web rose. "Before you are excused, Mister Hennessey, may I ask a few clarifying questions? In your experience, has the success rate of your work—the matching of fingerprints that you lift to those in the FBI files—been overwhelming?"

"Oh, objection," Bomber said. "Really, Web, it is not necessary to put words in Mister Hennessey's mouth. He's perfectly capable of testifying without being led."

"Mister Hanson, please," the judge said. "If you have an objection, address it to me."

"I object."

"Sustained."

"Mister Hennessey," Web continued, "how would you characterize the success ratio of fingerprinting in cases you are familiar with?"

Hennessey opened his mouth in the shape of an 'oh' as though to say 'overwhelming', then caught himself. "A very high success rate."

"Over ninety percent?"

"Easily."

"And for clarification, how many cases, approximately, are we talking about—cases you are familiar with?"

"Many hundreds."

"Thank you," Web said. "No more questions."

Bomber took another shot. "Mister Hennessey, is it possible you have a familiarity with some cases, without having a knowledge if the match of prints was made exactly?"

"I suppose."

"And is it possible in some cases for the supposed match to be erroneous and go unchallenged?"

"Not very likely."

"But *possible?*"

"I suppose."

"You suppose? Is it *possible?* Yes or no?"

"Yes, it's possible."

"And it would just make sense to an expert or anyone else that the smaller the percentage of the sample, the more chance for error in the identification?"

"Yes."

"And in this case your sample was around one-third of the thumb?"

"Yes."

"The *right* thumb of the defendant?" Bomber pressed.

"Yes."

"And can you explain why there was only one-third of a thumbprint on the syringe? Why no more of the defendant's prints or anyone else's?"

"It is difficult to get prints lifted in the best of circumstances. I can't speculate on this particular case."

"Could it be that someone else handled the syringe after whoever that one-third of a thumb belonged to?"

"Objection," the D.A. said. "Speculative."

"Sustained."

"Or that someone wearing gloves gave Easy Noggle the fatal injection with a syringe the defendant had previously handled?"

"Same objection."

"Sustained."

"No further questions."

The judge looked at the clock on the wall. "Who is your next witness, Mister Grainger?"

"Igor Sulwip."

"Will it be lengthy?"

"I expect it will."

"Let's break for lunch then. We can reconvene at one."

26

Igor 'Fingers' Sulwip was all suit as he sauntered down the aisle to take his place in the witness box. The suit was cheaply made and too large for him, as was the shirt, and yet he tugged at his shirt collar as though it were restricting him. It seemed to me Fingers was struggling to look like a man of the world—a guy whose word you could trust. The cheap, ill-fitting suit conspired against it. It reminded me of the difference between big-shot private attorneys, who could dress their nogoodnicks up in Brooks Brothers suits that made them look like orthopedic surgeons, and the state. The district attorney had a closet full of these suits for the jailhouse snitches, and none of them ever seemed to fit anybody.

Prince Igor, I said to myself as he held his head up and twisted in his suit to raise his hand to take the oath, promising to tell the truth, and nothing but the truth. Fat chance, I thought.

Prince Igor was an opera by Alexander Borodin, a Russian composer. It was written over many years, and completed by Rimsky-Korsakov and friends after Borodin died. The composer himself had been sired illegitimately by a prince, which I thought was a nice touch. The thought reminded me of how I had been slacking off on the composition I'd promised my beloved Joan I would write. I could, in that moment with Prince Igor lumbering to his witness chair, imagine a whole movement devoted to, well, Prince Igor's movements.

District Attorney Grainger stood between Igor 'Fingers' Sulwip and the jury—the standard place to be if you didn't want your witness scrutinized.

"Mister Sulwip, are you acquainted with the defendant

Melissa McHagarty?"

"Yes, sir."

"Could you tell the jury how you made her acquaintance?"

"Yeah, well, she called me up and said we should meet, it would be worth my while."

"Did you meet?"

"Yeah, sir."

"Where?"

"On Cornwell Street, in Teague's office."

"And that would be Attorney Foster Teague whose office is on Cornwell Street?"

"Yes."

"And how are you acquainted with Mister Teague?"

"He's married to my wife's sister."

"I see. Were there other people there?"

"Yes."

"How many?"

"I don't know. She had a man with her. Foster was there."

"What month?"

"Last July."

"That would be before Easy Noggle was murdered?"

"Yeah."

"What did she want from you?"

"She asked me how much I wanted to off her husband."

"Off?"

"Yeah—waste. You know—kill."

"What did you tell her?"

"That I didn't do that kind of work."

"What did she say?"

"Did I know anyone who did?"

"Did you?"

"No." He shook his head vigorously. It was a gesture I could see him rehearsing in front of a mirror. "I don't do hits."

"Did you ask Melissa McHagarty where she got the

idea you did?"

"Yeah."

"What did she tell you?"

"Nothin'. She wouldn't tell me."

"Now, Mister Sulwip, you are presently incarcerated, are you not?"

"Yes."

"What is the charge against you?"

"Robbery." Then more quietly he added, "Armed robbery."

Bomber couldn't resist. "I'm sorry, I didn't hear the last part of his answer. Could he repeat it?"

Fingers looked at Bomber, baffled. Then turned to Web who said, "Would you repeat it please?"

"Armed robbery," he said, as though the brief interval had given him the requisite courage.

Bomber nodded. "Thank you."

"And when were you incarcerated on that charge?"

"December twelfth, last year."

"How did you happen to tell me about Melissa McHagarty's approach to you to kill her husband?"

"After I hear she's arrested, I thought what happened between us was important—so I tells you about it."

"Where was that?"

"In your office."

"Do you remember when that was?"

"In August, last year."

"Approximately four months before you were arrested?"

"Yeah."

"Were you incarcerated at that time?"

"No, I wasn't."

"And had you agreed to testify when you told me about the defendant trying to hire you to kill her husband?"

"Yes."

"Why?"

"I dunno. It was the right thing. I had info about a

crime, so I came forward like a good citizen."

Bomber rolled his eyes and feigned a swoon for the jury. Web didn't see it.

"Did I promise you anything?"

Fingers couldn't wait to respond with his resounding, "No!"

"In exchange for your testimony?" Web got the rest of his question out after the answer had been given. The D.A. looked as if he felt a little foolish.

"No," Fingers answered again.

"And at that time, last August, did you have any matters pending before the court?"

"No, I did not."

"Did you ask me for anything in exchange for your testimony?"

"No, I did not."

"Did I hint or signal in any way that I might do some favor for you if you testified in court?"

"Your Honor," Bomber said, "with all due respect to our district attorney, who apparently favors God, country and motherhood, the question has been asked and answered, and beaten to death. Shakespeare said it best, 'the lady doth protest too much.'"

Now the judge was angry. He pounded his gavel as though trying to quiet an unruly courtroom crowd. "We'll have no more of that, Bomber. You know courtroom decorum as well as anyone. A simple objection will suffice—an outburst like that skirts contempt of court."

"I stand corrected," then after his bogus bow, he added, "but I still object."

"It's a more far reaching question," Web said in his defense.

"Yes, all right," Judge Pendegrast said, "let him answer."

"No," Fingers said. "No promises. No, how'd you say, signals. No nothin'."

"Thank you. Your witness."

"Thank *you*, Mister Prosecutor," Bomber said, rising. He stationed himself away from the jury so they might concentrate on the witness and his answers.

"Mister Sulwip," Bomber began his tone benignly, "do you have any aliases…or nicknames?"

The witness slumped in his chair, then straightened. "Some people used to call me Fingers."

"Fingers?" Bomber said in delighted surprise as though he had no prior knowledge of the name. "Why is that?"

Fingers shrugged. "I don't know."

"Come now, Fingers, you must have *some* idea. Where did you first hear yourself referred to as Fingers?"

"It might have been in…incarceration."

"Oh? What were you in jail for?"

"The charge was shoplifting—but I was innocent."

"No doubt," Bomber said, with heavy sarcasm.

"Your Honor," Web cut in, "please tell the defense attorney not to make snide comments to the witness."

"Yes, Mister Hanson. You know better."

"I stand corrected," Bomber said and ducked, of course, his head.

"So the Fingers nickname referred to the dexterity of your fingers?"

"Dex what?"

"Terity…dexterity—nimbleness, perhaps quick movements. I expect it was complimentary, like you could lift things from a store with ease—an artist," Bomber said, then after he saw Fingers smile, added, "of sorts."

"Yeah, well, but I was innocent."

Bomber made a big show to the jury of opening his mouth, then closing it, as though he were stifling the same sarcasm he was admonished for before. "Now, Fingers," Bomber paused for thought, "I take it you like the name?"

Fingers shrugged. "It's okay."

"Okay? Okay—I take it this current incarceration—is

that what the district attorney called it? Incarceration? Strike that," Bomber said, changing his mind. "You said you've been in prison before, Fingers, is that correct?"

"Yeah."

"How often?"

"May I object to that, Your Honor? Mister Sulwip is not on trial here."

"Oh, but his testimony is," Bomber said.

"All right, overruled."

"How often, Fingers, have you been in jail?"

"Counting the times there was no conviction?"

Bomber nodded, encouragingly. "Yes, sure."

"I guess about six, all told."

"Six?"

"About that."

"You aren't sure?"

"I'll stay with six."

"Very good," Bomber said, nodding his approval. "How many of those stays resulted in convictions?"

"Only two."

"So this present arrest, if convicted, could result in a third strike for you?"

"Could," Fingers acknowledged.

"Put you away for a long time?"

"Yeah. But nobody promised me nothin'."

I glanced at the jury. They were getting interested.

"Now, in those four cases where charges were dropped, was there any arrangement made with the district attorney's office to go easy in exchange for your help with other outstanding crimes?"

"I never made no deals."

"You didn't?"

"No."

"So those four arrests, which were not pressed to their natural conclusion, were simply a result of the police nabbing the wrong man?"

"I object, Your Honor," Web said, jumping to his feet as some of the jurors exchanged glances, "to Bomber ridiculing and belittling these proceedings."

"He has a point, Mister Hanson. Try to be more professional."

I could hear Bomber's imagined riposte. *I'm trying. I'm just not succeeding.*

"Do you understand the question, Fingers?"

"Yeah. They got the wrong man."

"False arrests?"

"Yeah."

"Ever sue the cops for false arrest?"

"Objection."

"Sustained."

"Very well," Bomber said, turning back to the witness. "Now, Fingers, are you what is known in your trade as a snitch?"

"No!"

"You've never testified for the prosecution before?"

"Objection," Web said. "Outside the scope of direct, irrelevant."

Judge Pendegrast's brow furrowed. "I think I'll allow it, overruled."

Bomber turned to Fingers. "Ever testify before?"

"I may have."

"For the prosecution against the defendant?"

"I guess so."

"How often?"

"Couple times."

"How many is a couple to you?"

"Well," he said as though that were a stupid question, "two."

"Three including this time?"

"Yeah."

"All right, thank you, Fingers."

The district attorney was on his feet. "Your Honor, I would request the court to admonish Mister Hanson to show the witness some respect by addressing him properly for this venue—I'm up to here with Fingers."

The judge looked at Bomber.

"And what name might that be?" Bomber asked Web— knowing full well what that might be.

"Mister Sulwip," Web obligingly replied.

"Would you prefer that, Fingers?" Bomber asked the witness, who shrugged. "Because I *do* want to put you at ease, and if calling you Mister instead of Fingers will do it, I will be only too happy to oblige."

Judge Pendegrast realized he had let Bomber run on too long. "All right, Bomber, call him Mister."

"Certainly, Your Honor," and turning to Fingers, said, "All right, Mister Sulwip. If I told you your car was seen at the scene of the crime in August, what would you say?"

Fingers, or Mr., Sulwip opened his mouth to answer, but before he could, Web had jumped up. "Objection! There's no foundation for that. Bomber's on a fishing expedition."

"Sustained."

"Okay—Mister Sulwip—have you ever driven your car to the residence of Doctor McHagarty?"

"I don't remember driving up there," he said, weakly.

"You don't *remember?*"

"No-o-oh," he said, then added a delightful clarifier: "A lot of people use my car."

"Who might have used it besides you on August eighteenth of last year, Mister Sulwip?"

"I have no idea."

"How many people use your car, Mister Sulwip?"

"Many."

"Ten thousand?"

"Not that many."

"Three?"

"More than that."

"Five?"

"More."

"Shall I keep going, Mister Sulwip, or will you give us a number?"

"Maybe between ten and fifteen."

"May we have some of the names?"

"I don't remember them all."

"I didn't ask for all of them, Mister Sulwip, just the ones you remember."

"Yeah, well, it varies."

"Varies? How?"

"Different people at different times."

"Just so, Mister Sulwip, can you give us some names?"

"Not offhand."

"If the court asked you to go back to your cell and write down those you remember who used your car, would you be able to produce some names, Mister Sulwip?"

He frowned. "I couldn't promise nothin'."

"How about the *reasons* so many people drive your car, Mister Sulwip?"

He shrugged. "Car's in the shop, saves a bus ride, errands."

"For you?"

"Mostly for them."

"Some for you, Mister Sulwip?"

He shrugged.

"Give an audible answer please, Mister Sulwip."

"Maybe."

"What kind of errands, Mister Sulwip?"

"I'll have to think about that."

"Go ahead," Bomber said. "Think, Mister Sulwip."

Bomber really overdid calling him Mister, and each time with just a touch of sarcasm, but not so much Web felt he could make an issue out of it. He had after all, requested, *insisted*, we call the witness Mister Sulwip—he could hardly object without looking silly. Besides, it didn't take a rocket scientist to see what Bomber was doing. He knew it. He did it anyway.

"Sorry, I just can't remember nothin' right now."

"If we took a recess, you think you might refresh your memory, Mister Sulwip?"

"Might," he said, without putting much hope in the tone.

"Perhaps your prison guard could call someone for you who could remind you?"

"Your Honor," Web stood again, "this is obviously subterfuge. If Bomber has a witness that can connect Mister Sulwip or his car to the crime, let him do so."

"Pleasure," said Bomber, "may we approach the bench?"

"Yes," the judge said, "but let's take a fifteen minute recess for the jury. Be back in fifteen minutes, ladies and gentlemen," the judge said, and we all watched them march out with their modest air meant to camouflage feelings of self-importance.

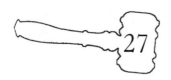

27

Web, Bomber and I stood before Judge Pendegrast's bench, with Bomber doing the talking.

"Web wants foundation for my questions about Fingers, ah, Mister, Sulwip's car at the crime scene. I have a witness to it, and I would like to offer a stipulation to the district attorney—if called, said witness will testify he saw such and such a car with license such and such registered to the witness, Igor Sulwip, on several dates which we will specify."

"On the day of the murder?"

"After."

Web threw up his hands. "What is the relevance?"

"I'd like to ask Mister Sulwip that," Bomber said. "If it is irrelevant, as Web suggests, there should be no objection. My client is charged with a capital crime, and I think this evidence creates doubt."

Web shook his head. "I don't buy it."

"I understand," Bomber said. "If Fingers Sulwip were one of my witnesses, I'd want to keep the questions to a minimum too."

Web's expression beseeched Judge Pendegrast for help.

"Who's the witness, Bomber?"

"One of my investigators."

Web looked at me. "Tod?" he said.

Bomber nodded.

"Well he's right here. He can testify."

The cold shivers zoomed through me again. With Bomber in the courtroom I'd be stammering all over the place, and I didn't see how he could remove himself without creating a scene.

"Yes he can," Bomber said. "I was just trying to simplify."

I could see the gears meshing in Web's head. He opened his mouth, and closed it again.

"Mister District Attorney?" the judge asked. "How say you?"

Web sayeth nothing.

Bomber spoke to the judge. "Perhaps he is remembering the last time he insisted Tod take a central role in a case. He thought Tod'd fall on his face, but it backfired. He was a triumph."

"I heard about that," the judge said. "Lot of good reports."

I ducked my head, not unlike Bomber when he says 'I stand corrected,' but I was sincere.

"Nonsense," Web said. "I have nothing to fear from the boy."

"All right," Bomber said.

"Then again, I have nothing against saving time. If Your Honor wants to receive the testimony, though I continue to object to it, why, a stipulation will be fine."

"Very well, if you give me the dates, I will read the stipulation." And I was mercifully off the hook.

When we sat back down, I asked Bomber, "How could you offer t-to th-throw me t-to the wolves like that?"

"I knew he'd go along after you blew him away last time."

Was Bomber really that confident in the outcome? I certainly wasn't.

"Now, what were those dates?"

I wrote down the information for Bomber—dates, make of car, license plate—and he took them to the judge. Then we left the courtroom for the remaining time of the recess.

When we got to the hall, Bomber said, "Well, what do

you think, me boy?"

I shrugged my shoulders rather than asking, think about what?

"I think we're creating some doubt. Maybe we'll put her on the stand. Doctor McHagarty versus Fingers Sulwip—no contest!"

Why was I uneasy? I'd pushed for him to take the case, but he was acting with uncharacteristic abandon. Erratic, I thought. You didn't switch game plans while the game was in progress. It wasn't prudent. Did Bomber, for instance, really want to place at the scene of the crime the man who claimed he had been approached to hit Easy Noggle by his wife, who admitted to a similar thought with a slightly different scenario?

Back in the courtroom, Fingers resumed the stand. I realize I should probably call him Mr. Sulwip, as the judge had ruled, but Fingers is just so darn colorful.

Judge Pendegrast read the stipulation about me seeing the car at Melissa's house after the murder. No one identifiable was seen at the car or house, either time.

Fingers received the information passively. Certainly Web had filled him in on the development.

"Now, ah, Mister Sulwip," Bomber let us all know his inclination was to call him Fingers, "did you visit the house of the defendant on either of the dates noted in the stipulation?"

"No."

"Do you have an explanation for your car being parked there, a block from the nearest house?"

"No, I don't. Like I said, a lot of people use my car."

"You *did* say that. Have you been able to recall any of their names?"

"Not really."

"Not really? Is that a yes, no, or maybe?"

"No."

"Come now, Mister Sulwip, tell us who drove your car to the Noggle house on those dates."

"I don't know."

"Well, who had access to your car and its keys on those dates?"

"I don't remember. It's a long time ago."

"How about a list of possibilities?"

"Can't think of any," then Fingers added what I thought was a nice touch, "Sorry."

"All right, Mister Sulwip, where were you on those dates?"

"I can't remember that."

"No? Well they were both weekdays. Do you have a regular routine on weekdays? Do you, for example, work in a bank?"

"I don't work no banks," Fingers protested and he brought down the house without understanding why.

"Too risky?" Bomber asked with a smile.

"Objection," Web was on his feet and red in the face. He didn't share the humor.

"Sustained."

"Well," Bomber resumed, "what *do* you do?"

"Do?"

"Yes. For an occupation—for a living."

Fingers shrugged. "Odd jobs."

"But not banks."

"Objection!" Web cried amid the laughter, but the judge was smiling in spite of all the efforts to hide his mirth.

"And I move it be stricken from the record."

"Lot of good that'll do," Bomber whispered to me and the jury.

"All right," Judge Pendegrast said when he brought himself and the audience under control, "strike it."

"Thank you," said Webster Arlington Grainger III, fearless district attorney of Weller County.

"Okay, Mister Sulwip, let me give you some names of people who might have used your car. Tell me if you know the person and if he or she has ever used your car."

Bomber began with a group of fictitious names. Fingers

said no to them all. Then Bomber began with known associations. "Foster Teague?"

"Yeah, I know him. I ought to, he's my wife's sister's husband." Was Fingers playing for laughs? If so, he had a mild success.

"So Foster Teague uses your car?"

"Maybe, sometimes."

I thought the slight gasp from Dr. McHagarty was the first reaction we'd gotten from her at the trial. I didn't understand why. It was, I hoped, probably not related to the witness.

"Does Mister Teague have a car of his own?"

"Yeah."

"But he could use your car?"

"I guess."

"Under what circumstances would he drive your car to Doctor McHagarty's house?"

"I wouldn't know about that."

Rather than confuse the jury with more names, Bomber let it go. "Now excuse me for dropping your occupation. There was some merriment, and I got sidetracked. I believe you said you did odd jobs. Could you be more specific?"

"Like handyman stuff."

"Some examples?"

"Fix leaking faucets, stopped up drains, stuck doors and windows, carpentry, plumbing, some electrical."

"Are you licensed for any of these activities?"

"Nah, I'm just a handy guy."

"Just so. Do you have any records of your work—bills and such?"

"I don't keep much records."

"So you don't have anything in writing that might have a date on it?"

"Not really. It's just casual labor."

"Do you pay income tax?"

"What?"

"Is that a 'what's income tax,' or you didn't hear or

understand the question?"

"Yeah, well, if I made enough money, I'd pay tax."

"Who do you let decide what's enough? You or the IRS?"

"Well, they have these categories."

"Your Honor," Web said, "I am going to have to object. We are getting so far afield here. This is not a tax trial."

"Mister Sulwip can be glad of that," Bomber said.

"Your Honor, there he goes again."

"Please, Mister Hanson, no more outbursts."

"I stand corrected. I am simply trying to tie Mister Sulwip to some activity to corroborate his statement that it was not he who drove his car to Doctor McHagarty's house. He isn't being much help."

"Well Mister Hanson," Judge Pendegrast said, "I don't see your line of questioning getting us anywhere."

"I'll agree to that. Let me wrap it up then. Mister Sulwip, may I sum up your car testimony thusly: you own a car, which you loan to many people—let them drive it—only you can't remember any of them?"

"Objection, asked and answered."

"Sustained."

"You work as a handyman but keep absolutely no record of your work."

"Same objection."

"Sustained."

"Mister Sulwip, you testified that Doctor McHagarty tried to hire you to kill her husband, is that correct?"

"Yes."

"But didn't she come to see you because you had been hired by her husband to kill her?"

Fingers shifted in his seat before he said—"No."

"There was a man with her when you met at a lawyer's office?"

"Yeah."

"And a police car at the curb—outside the window

where you could see it?"

"I didn't notice no police car."

"All right, Mister Sulwip—do you think Doctor McHagarty was making all these elaborate precautions because she was hiring you to kill someone, or was it more likely because she feared you were going to kill her? Why would she want witnesses if she were committing a felony?"

"Objection. Outside the scope of his knowledge."

"Sustained."

"Now, Mister Sulwip, you said you went to the district attorney of your own volition last August, soon after the murder of Easy Noggle."

"Yeah."

"And there were no promises made to you at that time."

"Yeah."

"And after that you were arrested and found yourself—" Bomber paused as though he were having trouble remembering the word—"incarcerated."

"Uh huh."

"Mister Sulwip," the judge said, "please answer yes or no. Uh huh could be misconstrued."

"Okay, yes."

"And now, when you *are* testifying you are…incarcerated?"

"Uh, yes."

"So, did the district attorney remind you of your conversation of six or so months ago? The one in which you testified Doctor McHagarty tried to hire you to kill her husband?"

"He might have."

"Come to see you in jail?"

"I believe so."

"So when you made the final deal to testify, you were in jail, incarcerated?"

"I think that's the way it finally came down."

"What are you going to get for your cooperation?"

"*Nothing!* No deals ever made."

"Oh? Just trying to live up to your reputation as a snitch?"

"Objection!"

"Sustained," said the judge, shooting an angry stare at Bomber.

"Mister Sulwip, do you have *any* thoughts of leniency in your sentencing because of your cooperation with the district attorney on this case?"

"No deals. He didn't promise me nothin'."

"Just so, I am speaking not of promises, but of hopes you have."

"Well, yeah, I guess you always hope."

"Thank you, Mister Sulwip, no more questions."

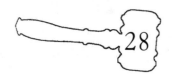

28

Henry Ziggenfoos, the drug salesman was in court every day. Before he was to testify, he stopped Bomber in the hall.

"I'm sorry the prosecution has called me as a witness. I'm on Melissa's side—I wouldn't do anything to hurt her."

"Good!" Bomber said.

"I know she didn't do it," he said. "She's under a lot of strain—you asking her to lie and say she did…"

"Hold on there a minute, pardner—" Bomber held his hand between them "—where you getting your information?"

"I visited Melissa in jail."

"Very nice," Bomber said. "I'm sure she appreciated it. I would appreciate if you were more careful how you characterize the attorney/client relationship."

"Oh," Ziggenfoos hung his head—"sorry. It's just…just that I'd do anything to save her."

"You would?" Bomber said. "Anything?"

"Yes—anything."

"Then confess to the crime yourself."

"Wha…b…but…I…didn't…"

While Henry Ziggenfoos was sputtering Bomber walked away.

I thought that was not one of Bomber's finest moments, but when Henry got on the stand as Web's witness, it was clear he was shaken up—so much so that though what he was testifying to was clearly true, it somehow seemed false.

Yes, he got an unusually large order for drugs of the feel good variety from Dr. McHagarty, but he thought nothing of it.

She was a wonderful person and doctor. That he was after all in the business of selling drugs—feed his family and all that...

Web had the order sheets from all Melissa's transactions, and the district attorney noted that the poison had come from Ziggenfoos.

"Well, I don't know that."

"Isn't it there on the order sheet?"

Bomber stood. "Your Honor, the witness apparently knows more about the rules of testimony than the district attorney does. There is no connection between the potassium cyanide on the order sheet and that in the victim's body. It is speculative, and I must, on behalf of my client, object to it."

"Sustained."

"All right, Mister Ziggenfoos, the defendant, Doctor McHagarty, ordered potassium cyanide from you?"

"Objection," Bomber said, "asked and answered."

"Sustained."

"And the victim was injected with potassium cyanide?"

"Objection. He's answered that. He heard that, not that he has independent knowledge of it."

"Sustained."

"But you *had* heard that?"

"Objection, asked and answered."

"Sustained."

"Oh, all right," Web said, not happy at the turn of events. He looked down at his notes for another question, but apparently decided he'd got all he could. "Your witness," he said.

The witness seemed relieved to have Bomber ask his softball questions about how long he had known the defendant (6 years), how many drugs he'd sold in his career (too many to count), what types? (*all* types). Habit forming? (yes), poisons even? (yes), aspirin (yes, can be the most lethal over-the-counter drug if taken in large quantities).

He told, over the prosecutors objections, Melissa was distraught, said she was doing it for her husband who was in

151

some financial difficulty and she did it only one time.

After Bomber finished with Henry Ziggenfoos, the prosecution rested. Bomber made the usual motion for the judge to throw out the case because the district attorney had not proven a prima facie case, but the judge thought otherwise, as they almost always do.

Court adjourned for the day. Bomber requested, and was granted, a meeting with his client in the conference room.

We settled in the conference room. The guard stood outside the door.

"Doctor," Bomber began, "they have just presented a strong but circumstantial case. I have decided with the makeup of the jury being what it is, you have a somewhat better chance by sticking to your original contention that you didn't do it."

"I didn't."

"Good," Bomber said without adding any inflection of true belief.

"But why did you change your mind?"

"The jury mostly. If we try to maintain you may well have been driven to it, I don't see a lot of sympathy on that panel. We didn't begin to get our demographics, and I don't think there is one person there who would be sympathetic. On the other hand, their case really has only two solid points—you bought the poison and the syringe was yours. Oh, and he apparently took the injection willingly. That's a stumbling block. Have you been able to think of anyone else who could give him a shot in the rear at his sufferance?"

She shook her head.

"What about this Foster Teague," Bomber asked, scrutinizing his client's face with care.

"He's not involved," Melissa said almost angrily.

"Is he a sore subject? I imagine he would be if he's the cause of your having to deal drugs."

"He's not! It was Easy's idea."

"Foster Teague didn't pressure him?"

"Not that I know of."

"Could Fingers Sulwip have leaned on him for payment?"

Melissa stared at him blankly.

"Apparently Foster Teague drove Mister Sulwip's car to your house."

Melissa said nothing. Was she telling us the whole story?

"Okay," Bomber said. "I just want you to understand what our pitfalls are. The injection, the syringe, and of course Fingers Sulwip denying Easy hired him to kill you. Since he *didn't* kill you, that may be difficult to refute. Of course, I can claim it was your getting wind of it that put him off. Doubtless you would have told someone, and Fingers would have been in the soup. It *is* your word against his, and on its face that should be a no-brainer. But you never know with some of the bozos we drew for that jury. I don't think that million dollar policy on his life will go away as an issue, either." Bomber sighed heavily.

"Guess it looks pretty bleak," she said.

"I've had more promising cases." Bomber brightened. "I only wish I could overcome this nagging feeling that you are keeping something from me."

Melissa said nothing.

"Are you holding something back?"

She shook her head, but it was as though she didn't have the courage to speak.

Then Bomber went over the questions he would ask her and asked her to give him the answers she would give in court. The soft spot in her testimony as far as I could determine was that she *had* considered killing Easy and saying someone must have taken her syringe and injected Easy without her having the slightest inkling who that someone could be.

"Okay," Bomber said. "I wish it were more believable. Let's just hope it flies. My sense is you are being less than candid about something, and I fear the jury will feel it too. Do you feel it, Tod?"

I had to say, "Yes." Single words I could often manage

in Bomber's presence without a stutter. Sometimes even two or three.

Melissa frowned.

"And I want to tell you," Bomber continued, "if a jury gets a sense someone isn't telling the whole truth, they just might decide that person is guilty, no matter how believable the rest of the story is. So I'd feel a lot better about this thing if you kept *nothing* from me. The analogy about one of your patients keeping something from you is still good. No matter what it is, if you really did kill him even, it is better for me to know so I can be prepared."

The lines in Melissa's forehead were getting deeper.

"One more thing. The sooner you tell me the better. So if you get religion in the middle of the night, insist on calling me."

"Oh, I couldn't do that."

"So call Tod instead. He's a light sleeper."

I wondered where he got that idea. Melissa said nothing. We said goodbye to her.

The red Bentley was in our sights. We were drawn to it automatically, without thought, like bees to pollen.

I suppose a psychiatrist would say it was obvious why Bomber went for the Chinese red Bentley instead of black or white—just as obvious as the reason for why I stutter in his presence alone, but I might not agree.

We drew closer to the car, gleaming like a hot sun in the afternoon, I asked Bomber, "What do you think sh-she is not t-telling you?"

"I think she gave him the shot. Maybe thought she was giving him testosterone or vitamins, and she's afraid if she admits *that* her goose *is* cooked. Lot more people could have switched the juice than could have given him a shot. The jury we have will never buy that someone else gave him the shot."

"Why d-didn't you tell her that?"

"I want her to come to it on her own. Lot stronger that way. More believable."

154

"Will you ask h-her on the stand?"

Bomber smiled a broad-as-Texas smile. We got in the Bentley for our four block drive back to the office. When we were both seated and he'd started the powerhouse engine, he said, "Well, me boy, I guess I'll just do what you musicians do."

"What?"

"Play it by ear."

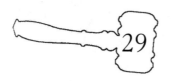

29

The case was in Bomber's hands. My work had been completed, and I felt a great load off my back. When I climbed the stairs to my room over the garage on the beach just south of Angelton, I felt as if I were floating up to the heavens.

When I opened the door and saw the little red light on my phone machine and heard my beloved Joan's voice, I was right up there with the gods.

"Hi, Barrister, I hope you're as happy as I am. I'm coming home to see you and I can't wait. Touring with an orchestra is grueling, and I'm looking forward to some R and R with you. Written any music for us? I'm dying to play with you. See you day after tomorrow. Love you."

Wow! My heart revved up to high gear and astronomical RPMs. I *had* to complete my Sonata for violin and piano, and I had one night and one day to do it. I had made only a few sketches, so I sat right down at the piano and, with thoughts of Joan flooding my brain, began to work at a fevered pitch.

By 3:30 a.m. I had a pretty good first draft. I was so exhilarated I couldn't sleep. I kept hearing the melodies and biting rhythms which set the tone of uncertainty in the piece. I decided to call it *An Easy Piece*.

I must have fallen asleep around five and was jolted awake by the alarm at seven. Though I always aspired to be able to get by on only a couple hours of sleep, I had not accomplished that. I only hoped nothing out of the ordinary would be required of me that day. I also hoped the adrenaline would keep me upright.

I met Bomber at the courthouse—the big old white Spanish number that never failed to inspire me upon entering it.

Bomber called Foster Teague to the stand.

"Mister Teague, when did you first meet the defendant?"

"Oh, about three or four years ago."

"What were the circumstances?"

"I went to see her as a doctor. I had been referred by a friend."

"Who was that friend?"

He thought a moment. "You know, it may have been my wife's sister."

"Mrs. Igor Sulwip?"

"Yes."

"She went to her, did she? For medical purposes?"

"I'm not clear on that. Sorry, I just don't remember for sure."

"What line of work are you in, Mister Teague?"

"I'm a lawyer."

"Nothing to be ashamed of," Bomber said, and got a chuckle for his efforts.

"Have you been back to see Doctor McHagarty professionally?"

"No."

"Why not?"

"I haven't been sick."

"Was the experience good?"

"Oh, yes."

"Would you recommend her to your friends?"

"Oh, yes."

"Was Doctor McHagarty married when you saw her in her office?"

"I really don't know."

"Were you acquainted with Fred—Easy Noggle, her husband?"

"Yes."

"In what capacity?"

"He approached me from time to time with business propositions."

"Did you enter into any business deals with Easy Noggle?"

"Not until I got him a loan on his house."

"What kind of loan?"

"A third trust deed."

"Would you explain what a third trust deed is?"

"Well, the first loan made on a property is usually the main one, the highest amount of money. That's the first trust deed. If that isn't enough money for a buyer or person who is financing, a second trust deed is taken. Usually a considerably lesser amount than the first. If the second isn't enough, a third could be taken."

"How does the rate of interest and risk compare?"

"The lower the loan position the higher the interest and greater the risk."

"Why is that?"

"If the trustee or borrower defaults, each lender has to cure the defaults of those ahead of him. So if I hold a third trust deed and the borrower doesn't pay the first or second, I have to pay them, and usually back taxes, or lose my investment."

"Did that happen with the loan in question? To Easy Noggle?"

"Yes."

"What was the amount of your loan?'

"A million dollars."

"What was the amount of the first trust deed?"

"Around four million. I believe three point eight or something like that, originally. With the back payments it is now around four million or so."

"And the second trust deed?"

"It was five hundred thousand. Now around thirty

thousand more is due on that."

"So you have roughly four point five million outstanding on the first and second. How about the taxes? Are they current?"

"No, there's about eighty thousand there."

"Okay, so there's, let's say, four point seven million, and you are owed a million and interest. What does it all add up to?"

"Around five point eight million."

"What can you sell the house for?"

"Not that much. Maybe five million—probably less after commission and costs."

I waited for Bomber to drop a bomb. The jury was getting sleepy, but nothing fell.

Then I realized Bomber was putting Foster Teague to sleep, though what he wanted to shock out of him, I couldn't imagine.

"Now, Mister Teague, you said you loaned money with the house on Hilltop as collateral, is that correct?"

"Yes."

"Does someone inspect the property before you commit to making the loan?"

"Yes."

"Who was that?"

"I did."

"When was that?"

"A few years ago, I can't pinpoint it. It was just before the house was completed."

"How often did you go there before you made the loan?"

"Just once."

"Was Easy at the house on that date?"

"No." Foster Teague said, then seemed to think a lawyerly clarification was necessary. "At least I didn't see him."

"Was Doctor McHagarty—Mrs. Noggle—there?"

"I believe she was."

"Did you speak to her?"

Foster Teague's brow scrunched. "I'm sure I did."

"Why are you sure?"

"Well, I had gone to her as a doctor, I hope I didn't ignore her."

"Correct me if I'm wrong, Attorney Teague, but didn't you testify that you saw Doctor McHagarty only once?"

"Did I? I don't believe so. I saw her only once professionally…as a patient."

"Yes, sorry. I think that's correct. I'll accept it at any rate. Then how often *have* you seen the defendant, Doctor McHagarty?"

"She came to my office seeking legal advice."

"When was that?"

"Perhaps a year or two into her marriage."

"Can you tell us the nature of that relationship?"

Teague shifted in his chair. "I would plead attorney-client privileged conversation."

"If your client agreed you could disclose the nature of the meeting, would you agree?"

"I suppose," he said, not looking too keen on it.

To Bomber's credit, he didn't turn to Melissa for her permission, but moved on.

"Have you seen the defendant since then?"

"Yes."

"What were the circumstances?"

"I called her to tell her I had news I thought I should give her in person. She came to my office and I told her. I'd heard Easy, her husband, tried to hire Fingers Sulwip to kill her."

The murmur from the courtroom was most gratifying to Bomber. He nodded, let it sink in, then asked, "What did she say?"

"She didn't want to believe it."

"Why did you tell her? I mean, wasn't Fingers Sulwip

your brother-in-law?"

"Well, yes, but I couldn't let him murder her."

"What did you say to him?"

"Not to do it, of course. I knew about it. Others must too, he would never get away with it."

"Why wouldn't you warn Melissa?"

"I did. I suggested she plead with him not to kill her."

"You weren't afraid he would murder her when they met?"

"No."

"Why not?"

"Those things are not done with witnesses."

"As far as you know, did she meet him?"

"Yes."

"Did Fingers or Melissa tell you anything about the meeting?"

"Fingers said she asked him not to do it."

"Did he say she tried to get him to kill Easy?"

"No."

"Did he say he was going to go through with his contract on her life?"

"No."

"Did he say he was *not* going to kill her?"

"No."

"You didn't ask?"

"I try to keep my contact with Fingers to a minimum. He is something of an embarrassment to the family."

"Why is that?"

"He has a criminal record."

"Thank you," Bomber said. "Have you been to the Noggle/McHagarty house in the last two months?"

"Yes."

"What was the nature of your visit?"

"I was inventorying the personal property."

"Why?'

"The house was in foreclosure, and I wanted to see if there was anything worth selling—cut my losses."

"How did you get to the house?"

Foster Teague looked confused. As if he didn't understand the question. "I drove."

"Your car?"

"Well, yes..." then he frowned. "No, coming to think of it, I borrowed a car."

"Whose?"

"My brother-in-law's."

"Is that Fingers Sulwip?'

"Yes."

"Did you often drive his car?"

"I think that was the first time."

"And why did you drive Finger Sulwip's car on that day?"

"Mine was being worked on, I believe."

"What was being done?"

"A ten-thousand mile check."

"And you didn't want to wait until you got your car back to make the trip?"

"The sale was approaching," he shrugged.

"On what other occasions did you drive Fingers Sulwip's car?"

"I can't think of any."

"Where was your car being worked on?"

"Haus Mercedes, over on Garden Street."

"Your car is a Mercedes?"

"Yes."

"What model?"

"CL six hundred."

"Is that the top of the line?"

"Next to the limousines."

"So if it was a ten-thousand mile check, it must be rather new."

"Well, it's ten-thousand miles new."

Bomber sat down and made a show of going through his notes, paging through his yellow legal tablet laboriously. While he did so he made a show of making notes. What he was doing was surreptitiously and casually making me a note, a little at a time:

> Check Haus Mercedes. Was
> car there on the date you saw
> him at Melissa's? Wait a while
> to leave. I'll stall him.

Bomber got to a page and feigned finding what he was looking for. He stood back up. He asked a few more sleeper questions, then, "How did you get Fingers' car that day?"

"His wife met me at Haus with it. I dropped her at work and drove it."

"What happened to the car when you left the house of the defendant?"

"I parked it behind my office."

"Was Fingers' car parked behind your office on other occasions?"

"Not to my knowledge."

"Did he ever visit your office building?"

"Oh, I suppose. He might park behind the office on those occasions."

"How often?"

"Seldom."

That was when I left the questioning. Haus Mercedes was walking distance from the courthouse. I hoofed it.

Hans of Haus Mercedes was an affable guy. Pretty clean uniform for a car mechanic. I introduced myself and said, "Foster Teague is trying to remember the date of his last appointment here. He's in court now."

"Good old Foster, haven't seen him in a while. Let me

look up exactly...."

I followed him into his compact office to the side of his four door garage. He pulled a file drawer out and then withdrew a file, which he opened and laid on the open drawer. "A five-thousand mile check," he said, and gave me a date a month before the date Foster Teague claimed.

I thanked him and the phone rang. I started out of the office, mouthed a thank you, and saw him frown at the phone.

"But...but," he said, "he's here now—said you were *looking* for the date."

I slunk out of there to hear Hans shout at my back, "You lied to me!"

I didn't wait for the rest of the tongue lashing.

When I got back to the courthouse, sure enough there was a recess.

Bomber explained it. Web caught on and pushed the recess. "Claimed it was a bathroom emergency. The judge said it was time anyway. What did you find out?"

"Teague wasn't there. Got a f-five-thousand mile ch-check a month before, and he c-called while I was there."

"I suppose to tell him not to tell you anything."

"Right. Hans f-flushed and c-claimed I t-tricked him."

"That's what Teague said when he figured it out."

"Angry?"

"You might say that," Bomber frowned. "I asked Melissa if she knew any reason he might have for fudging the truth."

"Wh-what did she s-say?"

He shook his head. "Said she didn't know of any."

"Believe her?"

"Of course not."

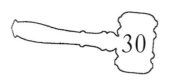

30

Court resumed with a wary Foster Teague back on the stand. He had begun as a friendly witness, but turned on Bomber's trick. The district attorney quickly and easily won him over by asking for the recess. Too bad for Teague it was a few seconds too late.

The change didn't seem to bother Bomber, and he continued as though nothing had changed. He could have declared Teague a hostile witness, but Bomber, as usual, was sublimely confident.

"Mister Teague, would you consider yourself mainly a loan broker, or a lawyer?"

"A lawyer," he answered lawyerly, without any extra information.

"How frequently do you make loans?"

"Perhaps one or two a month."

"Directing your attention to the loan you made to Easy Noggle, I believe you said it was for a million dollars, and you probably couldn't sell the foreclosed property and recoup your losses. Is that correct?"

"Yes."

"Can you tell the jury how you charge for a loan like that?"

"Well, a third trust deed is very unusual. We make more seconds. As I said before, the further down the line you are, the more onerous the terms."

"Onerous?" Bomber clarified. "Stringent? Tougher?"

"Yes."

"Higher interest?"

"Yes."

"Higher costs?"

"Yes."

"What was your agreement with Easy Noggle—interest rate and costs?"

"Twenty percent interest and twenty points."

"But, isn't that usury?"

"No. I am a real estate broker by virtue of my lawyer's license, and I am loaning money on real property. Twenty percent interest for a loan of this risk is not out of line."

"Usury laws have loopholes?"

"Like all other laws."

"Can you explain the twenty points?"

Foster Teague shrugged. "The risk."

"No, I mean tell the jury what points are."

"A loan fee. Twenty points is twenty percent of the face amount of the loan."

"What are the other costs?"

"Appraisal fee, documents, escrow, notaries, miscellaneous—title, policies, tax service."

"All told, what were the fees on Easy's loan?"

"Works out to somewhere around twenty-two percent or so."

"How much money is that?"

"Two hundred twenty thousand on a million dollar loan."

"How does he pay that? Write you a check?"

"It's deducted from the loan proceeds."

"So he borrows a million, but only gets seven hundred some thousand?"

"Around seven hundred eighty."

Bomber worked his eyebrows. "Phew," he said, "and you say you consider yourself a lawyer instead of a loan broker?"

"Well, it's fine if it works out. This time we had a major default, so what looks like a financial killing was really a major loss."

"What sort of entity do you have for lending?"

"Limited partnership."

"Please explain a limited partnership. How does it work?"

"The partners buy shares in the partnership. The limited partners limit their liability. In our case they can't lose more than their original investment."

"Which would be the amount they put up—or loaned?"

"Yes."

"But they could lose all of it?"

"Yes."

"And in this case may well have?"

"Yes."

"You were a general partner on the Easy Noggle loan?"

"Yes."

"Who were the limited partners?"

Foster Teague looked at Web as though he were his lawyer and could get him out of this mess.

"I don't recall all of them."

"How many were there?"

"I don't recall."

"Can you estimate?"

"Perhaps twenty to thirty."

"Do you put money in personally?"

"No, my partnership is earned by my organizing, securing the investors and managing the payments."

"So you didn't lose any money personally with the Easy Noggle limited partnership?"

"No."

"Were some of your partners angry that they lost their money?"

"Yes."

"Angry at you?"

"Some, I suppose."

"Would you be able to produce a list of those names for us this afternoon?"

Web stood and asked to approach the bench. Once we three were there, the district attorney began. "Your Honor, I am mystified by this behavior. This is *Bomber's* witness, why is he asking him on the stand for documents that he could have gotten before?"

"He is my witness," Bomber said, "but you must see how he has suddenly become a hostile one. We checked on his testimony about not driving Fingers Sulwip's car to the murder scene and found he was lying. Many avenues have opened up and perhaps if I had had more than a month to prepare my case, I would have smoked out these names of investors. But he's expressed his reluctance to provide the names for us, so I was about to petition the court to direct him to do so. I doubt we will get it otherwise."

"Your Honor, this is another delaying fishing expedition. Who does he think he'll find on the list—the murderer?"

"It's certainly possible that someone who loaned Easy money could have been involved in his murder. I am trying, with limited time, to be conscientious on my client's behalf. It seems to me a simple enough request."

"All right," the judge said. "So moved." The judge turned to Foster Teague on the stand. "Mister Teague, will you please produce for the court the records of your investors in the Fred Noggle property on Hilltop?"

"Your Honor, time is of the essence," said Bomber. "I could have my associate, Tod, return with Foster Teague to his office to pick it up."

"All right, Mister Teague, would you be able to comply with that request? Your counsel will facilitate returning it to this court. You may resume your questioning, Mister Hanson."

"Thank you, Your Honor." Bomber turned to face the

witness.

"You recall your testimony about borrowing a car registered to Igor, a.k.a. Fingers, Sulwip?"

Foster Teague frowned. "I may have been confused."

"But you recall the questions and answers?"

"Yes."

"I believe you said you borrowed his car because you took yours to the shop. Haus Mercedes, is that correct?"

"To the best of my recollection."

"Have you since had reason to recant that testimony?"

"Your Honor," Web said, "I object. This has no relevance whatsoever to the case."

"He may answer. Overruled. Veracity of the witness."

"You mean because your boy went snooping around the shop?"

"That is, of course, objectionable," Bomber said, "which you as an attorney must surely know, but I won't quibble with your characterization of investigation as snooping. Perhaps in your shoes I'd try to downgrade it too."

"Objection," Web said.

"Sustained."

"I move it be stricken from the record," said an outraged Web. "This ceaseless editorializing merits strong censure from the court in the prosecution's opinion."

"It will be stricken. Mister Hanson, *please* get hold of yourself."

"I stand corrected. Okay, Mister Teague, did you or did you not take your car for a ten thousand mile service to Haus Mercedes on October thirtieth, and subsequently drive Fingers Sulwip's car to the home of Fred Noggle and Doctor McHagarty?"

"As I recall the incident, that is what happened."

Web stood. "Your Honor, what does any of this matter?"

"Are you objecting?"

"Yes, Your Honor. I object."

"Overruled."

"Thank you, Your Honor," Bomber said with a bow of gratitude. "One more question on the subject, Mister Teague. Why would you get a ten-thousand mile check on a car with eighty-four hundred miles on it?"

There was a stunned silence in the courtroom. Even the jury registered it.

Web said, "Objection, Your Honor—without foundation," but it seemed he was embarrassed to do so.

The judge nodded thoughtfully, then turned to the witness. "Do you know how many miles your car has on it?"

"I honestly don't, Your Honor. Maybe it was a seventy-five hundred mile check. I don't keep close track of those things."

"You may proceed, Mister Hanson."

"Was there anything wrong with your car when you took it to Haus Mercedes? The Mercedes CL six hundred?"

"No, it was a routine check."

Bomber turned to the table—and scrawled a note for me:

Get Merc. serv. manual for his model.

"Mister Teague, were you in the armed forces at all?"

"Yes."

"When was that?"

"Between college and law school. That's about twenty-three or four years ago now."

"What branch of the service were you in?"

"The Navy."

"What was your specialty?"

The glare that passed between the witness and his examiner was hot enough to melt a diamond. "I was a pharmacist's mate," he said with reluctance.

"What did that work entail?"

"Filling prescriptions for drugs, mostly."

"Any habit forming drugs?"

"No."

"Any controlled substances?"

"Depends on the definition. There were definitely things you couldn't buy without a prescription."

Ever so casually, Bomber asked, "Did you handle drugs for the doctors?"

"Yes."

"Some taken orally?"

"Yes."

"Some injected?"

There was a beat—not very long in duration, but much too long in jury psychology before he said, "Yes."

"In the course of your duties, did you ever fill a syringe from a vial of some drug, say?"

"Occasionally," Teague said, reluctantly.

"But, you know how to do it?"

"Yes."

"How to fill a syringe with a drug?"

"Yes." Teague's eyes were narrowing.

"And, in the course of those duties, did you ever inject a patient?"

Teague answered slowly, deliberately, as if his careful answer would mislead some jurors. "I had advanced to the point where I was giving routine shots."

"Thank you, Mister Teague. No further questions."

Web stood. "Just a few clarifying questions, Mister Teague, if you will."

Foster Teague looked relieved, as though he belonged heart and soul to the prosecution, rather than to our side.

"Did you ever give Easy Noggle an injection?"

"No, I did not."

"Did you kill Easy Noggle?"

"No, sir!"

"Were you at his house on August eighteen of last year?"

"I was not."

Web looked at the jury and held his pose for a few seconds before he said, "No more questions."

Judge Pendegrast instructed Foster Teague to produce the list of investors in the loan on Easy Noggle's house by two o'clock that afternoon. I would come to his office to pick it up.

I expressed suspicion that he might change the list, but Bomber said a lawyer would not risk disbarment and possibly jail for so trivial a result. "Who could he protect, and why?" he asked. "By the way, let's get Hans Holbin to testify. Subpoena if you must."

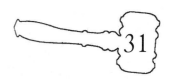

31

I managed to get Hans Holbin to court without a subpoena, and I put our dingbat secretary Bonnie Doone on the task of getting a service manual for Teague's Mercedes.

Hans Holbin was sworn in, and Bomber began with a snarl.

"You didn't want to come here, did you Mister Holbin?"

"Objection," said a weary Web

"Okay, did you want to come here, Mister Holbin?"

"Noooh."

"Why not?"

"I have a business to run. It costs me money I can't afford. I don't want to make trouble over no misunderstanding."

"What misunderstanding?"

"Foster and his bringing his car."

"What about his car?"

"I thought your man," he pointed at me at the defendant's table, "was coming to help Foster out."

"You referring to Foster Teague?"

"That's right."

"You do his automotive maintenance work, do you?"

"Yeah."

"What kind of car does Mister Teague bring you?"

"A Mercedes. I only do Mercedes." He pronounced it Mert *say* dis, as the owner's manual instructs one to do. I wondered if they still did that since joining up with Chrysler.

"What model?"

"CL six hundred."

"Just out of curiosity, what do those retail for?"

Hans Holbin shrugged. "Around one hundred twenty-five grand." Web must have been curious too, for he didn't object.

"All right, Mister Holbin, Foster Teague testified in court that his sister-in-law dropped him off at your place of business on October thirtieth, last year. My investigator, Tod Hanson at the table here," Bomber was standing behind me now, "came to your place to verify that yesterday. Do you remember that?"

"How could I forget it?"

"I don't know how, but with the attitude you display here I suspect you'd like to find a way."

"Oh, Your Honor," Web said, "he's badgering his own witness."

"I'll withdraw it."

"You know better," Judge Pendegrast said.

"I stand corrected."

I looked at the jury. They weren't buying his I-stand-correcteds.

"Did you tell Tod that Foster Teague had not been to your place on that day?" continued Bomber.

"I had to look it up."

"And when you looked it up, what did you find?"

"I found my records were a mess. If Foster Teague said he was there that day, I must have misfiled his paperwork. Foster Teague doesn't lie."

"Thank you, but I didn't ask that. The record will speak for itself. Did you not shout after Tod Hanson, 'You lied to me'?"

"I may have."

"How did he lie to you?"

"He misrepresented his relationship with Mister Teague."

"How did he do that?"

"Said he represented him."

"And you don't think he did?"

"Not after I talked to Mister Teague on the phone."

"When was that?"

"Just as your boy was leaving."

"You're referring to Tod here?"

"Yeah."

"Who called whom?"

"Foster called me."

"While he was still testifying in court?"

"Said he had a break."

"So why did he call you?"

"To straighten me out. To remind me he was there that day. I had just forgotten."

"Do you have any fear of Foster Teague?"

"No, why should I?"

"That's what I'm trying to find out. I ask the questions here, Mister Holbin. And under these peculiar circumstances I see no reason for changing your story other than fear."

"Objection."

"Sustained."

"Okay, I'll just recite the testimony and the facts, and you tell me when I am wrong."

"Objection."

"Oh," Judge Pendegrast said, "let him do it. Let's move on."

"Thank you, Your Honor. Yesterday my son and associate, Tod Hanson, came to your shop, Mister Holbin. He told you Foster Teague was on the stand for our side and wanted to clarify the date he brought his Mercedes to you."

"Yeah, well, that's not right."

"All right, correct the part that's wrong."

"That business about clarify. I think he was sneaky about how he said that."

"Said what?"

"I don't remember exactly."

"All right, what was the sense of it?"

"It was a misunderstanding. Tod Hanson made it seem Foster wanted me to give him the information, and then Foster called to tell me *not* to give it."

"But you had already given it, had you not?"

"Yeah, but it turns out I was wrong."

"How were you wrong? Didn't you pull a record from your files and give Tod a date from the record some one month prior to the date given by Foster?"

"A misunderstanding."

"And the record said it was a five-thousand mile check, not a ten-thousand as Mister Teague testified, correct?"

"I forgot which it was."

"Are you familiar with the perjury laws?"

"I guess."

"I'll refresh your memory. Lie in court, go to jail," Bomber said. "Now tell us, are you saying your records are wrong or you are?"

"I don't lie. I might forget. I might have my records wrong. I don't lie."

"That's a nice, self-serving declaration, Mister Holbin, but that is a judgment we'll let the jury make," Bomber said. "Your witness, Mister Prosecutor."

Web stood. "Mister Holbin, how many different cars have you serviced in your career?"

"I don't know—thousands."

"Do you remember when each of them came by for what kind of service?"

"No," he laughed with relief at the friendly questions.

"You keep records of these services, do you?"

"I try," he said. "I'm not good with records."

"What do you mean? Be specific if you can."

"Oh, I'll put some in the wrong folders, toss some by mistake, clean out my files now and then. My filing space is limited. I'm just not as careful as I guess I should be with my paperwork."

"So how do you explain this mix-up with Mister Teague's car service?"

"I misfiled the papers."

"Did you ever find them?"

"Yes."

"Did you bring them with you?"

"Yes."

"May we see them?"

He whipped out one of his forms. Web had it introduced into evidence. He went over the paperwork with the witness: the date, type of service and paid by cash notation. When we were given our copy we noticed Hans had written 7,500 mile service.

When Bomber got his turn, he asked, "Did anyone ever lie to you, Mister Holbin?"

"Well, your son did. Foster Teague, never."

"Anyone else?"

He shrugged. "I wouldn't know."

"Can you tell the jury how the ten-thousand mile service was changed to seventy-five hundred?"

"The invoice speaks for itself," he said.

"When did you make this invoice, Mister Holbin?"

"What's the date on it?"

"Does that matter?"

"That's when I wrote it up."

"Not yesterday?"

"No."

"Or today?"

"No."

"You *do* remember the perjury rules."

"Yeah, sure."

"Now, isn't it just possible you made this new one up to replace the one you mislaid?"

Holbin's eyes widened, then narrowed. He was being given an out, but wasn't sure he should take it. It could be a trap.

"I made it out when he brought the car."

"Did he bring the car yesterday or today?"

"Nah—the date's on the invoice."

"Do you make these invoices in order? I see there is a number at the top."

"Yeah, well," he squirmed, "as I said, I'm not good with paperwork, so I just grab what book is handy, and if the number is out of order, that's the reason."

"Oh, is the number out of order?" asked Bomber, the soul of innocence. "How many numbers is it off?" Bomber said, bobbing his head up and down. "No more questions."

"Mister Grainger?" Judge Pendegrast said.

"Just a few, Your Honor," Web stood and buttoned his suit jacket. "Mister Holbin, did you know Easy or Fred Noggle?"

"I heard of him. I never met him."

"Did you ever discuss Mister Noggle with Mister Teague?"

"No."

"Did Mister Teague ever mention his name to you?"

"No."

"Do you have any reason to suspect Foster Teague was in any way involved in Mister Noggle's murder?"

"Objection," Bomber said. "Calls for conclusion."

"Sustained."

"Did Foster Teague tell you he was borrowing Igor Sulwip's car?"

"No."

"In your business dealing with Foster Teague, has he always been up front and honest with you?"

"He's aces with me."

"Pay his bills?"

"Always. He's one of the best guys I ever met."

"No more questions."

"Character witness for a witness," Bomber whispered. "He needs it."

Bonnie Doone came breezing into the courtroom, and all eyes swiveled to her as though they were ball bearings and she was a magnet, which she was. She gave Bomber the Mercedes service manual and threw me a too-broad wink. Bomber asked to introduce it into evidence. Web objected. We held a bench conference. Web began:

"But why do you want to make a liar out of your own witness?" Web asked.

"Hostile, Web, ever hear of a hostile witness?"

"All right, gentlemen," Judge Pendegrast said. "I will allow it."

Back on the stand, Bomber showed the booklet to the witness and asked him, "Can you identify this booklet?"

He peered at it. "That's the service book for the CL six hundred."

"Will you look at it and tell us when the first required service is?"

"One thousand miles."

"And the second?"

"Five thousand."

"Third?"

"Ten thousand."

"Just so," Bomber said. "Now, will you point to the page that calls out the seventy-five hundred mile service you wrote up on your invoice?"

Holbin frowned. "I don't see it."

"Isn't there, is it?"

"No."

"Other than outright deception of this court and jury, can you think of any reason to perpetuate this fraud?"

Web jumped up. "Objection, Your Honor, he's badgering."

"Sustained."

"Did you just make up the seventy-five hundred mile check to fit Foster Teague's testimony?"

"No, I—"

"You what?"

"Foster is finicky about his cars. He hears a murmur, he brings it in."

"Is that what he did?"

"As best I can recall."

"So why didn't you write it up as a repair?"

He shrugged. "I don't know."

"No more questions."

"Any questions, Mister Grainger?"

"I think this dead horse needs a rest," he said. "No more questions."

"Now, who's speechifying?" Bomber whispered—this one good for the whole courtroom.

"Are we finished with this witness, gentlemen?"

"Yes, Your Honor," both counsel answered in unison.

"Very well. You may go, Mister Holbin."

When the judge declared the lunch recess and the jury filed out, Dr. McHagarty leaned over, put her hand on Bomber's arm, and whispered, "I have to talk to you."

Bomber feigned a surprise I don't think he felt, then faced the judge, stood, and said, "Your Honor, I respectfully request the use of the conference room for a meeting with my client."

"Granted. Bailiff, escort the defendant to the conference room, please."

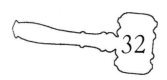

32

Even before we got to the conference room there was no doubt Melissa was agitated. It was Bomber's policy—when he could stick to it—not to let on he knew someone was upset until he heard what he had to say.

"Always listen first," he'd told me on more than one occasion, "because often your assumptions are wrong."

"Doctor, what are your feelings so far about the trial?"

Melissa seemed stunned by the question. "You're the expert on trials." Her answer was curt. "I wouldn't know."

"You are still comfortable with our approach that you are innocent of the charges?"

"Yesss," she said so tentatively it could have meant anything.

She had pushed Bomber over the edge. "Now, young lady, out with it. What are you hiding?"

"Nothing," she said so weakly she was signaling, throwing her arms out for help, as though sinking in a strong undertow.

"Are you afraid of Foster Teague?"

"No...yes...no...I don't know."

"You gave Easy the shot, didn't you?"

"No...yes...no...I don't remember."

"Remember!"

"I gave him shots every week," she said, miserable at the memory.

"What kind of shots?"

"Vitamins, testosterone."

"So how did he get the cyanide?"

"I don't know."

"Did you put it in the syringe?"

She frowned. "I don't...think so."

Melissa sounded hopelessly confused, like the memory was too painful or too incriminating. I didn't envy Bomber having to defend such a confused, conflicted and chimerical client. *My* client! They went back and forth, and I could hardly make sense of the dialogue.

"How about this Foster Teague?" Bomber asked. "Any possibility?"

I can't speak for Bomber, but to me she looked startled. There was no jerking of the body or anything, it was all in her face—a flicker of the eye, a slight tensing of the lips.

"Possibility?" she said as though confused, "possibility of what?"

"For switching syringes. For filling it with cyanide."

"No, oh no," she said.

"No what?"

"He could never give him the injection. Easy would not have sat still for it. And switching the syringe, how could he? How would he? I mean he's a lawyer, not a hardened criminal."

"Thank you for that," Bomber said. "Lot of folks can't tell the difference."

I laughed. Melissa didn't. She looked nervous.

"All right, Melissa, do you want to testify?"

"Which way would my chances be better?" she asked.

"Hard to tell. It depends a lot on how convincing you are. If you're able to stick to your guns, even when the prosecutor comes at you with a nuclear bomb, you may have a shot. My sense of the jury is still not favorable. If you aren't convincing, my guess would be we'd lose. So my order of preference is you give a zinger textbook quality, honest, convincing testimony, both on direct and cross examination, and I follow with a convincing argument that plants solid doubt in the minds of the jurors. My second choice is to go it alone and take my chances. The last option I think would sink us. You get on the stand, lie and tell a story without conviction. You aren't going to say, for example, that you gave him a shot *and* you put the poison in the syringe? You just forgot?"

She shook her head.

"Okay—what do you say? Testify or not?"

"Testify," she said.

But Bomber needed more time to go over Melissa's testimony, so when the recess ended he asked the judge for the rest of the afternoon to prepare.

Web balked. He saw victory within his grasp, and he wasn't about to let it slip away with unwanted delays.

The judge was also skeptical. "This could hardly have come as a surprise to you, Bomber," Judge Pendegrast said to Web, Bomber and me, assembled before him, the jury not yet returned.

"Foster Teague's testimony was a surprise."

"A mirage, a goose chase," Web said. "He is *your* witness."

"Doubt," Bomber said. "We are changing the thrust of our defense to not guilty by virtue of pure innocence."

"You don't have to get so flowery for me," Judge Pendegrast said.

"Amen," Web said.

"Well," Bomber concluded, "I need the time. I think it is vital to my client's defense, and I think her interests will be grossly prejudiced if we are forced to proceed without proper preparation. I don't have to remind you we came on board here at the last minute."

"You had a month," Web said.

"One month to mount a murder defense!" Bomber snorted, looking at the stenographer's fingers dancing on the compact keyboard of her steno machine. "The public defenders get *more than one month!*"

Bomber's not so subtle glance at the stenographer's

machinations signaled the judge if he ruled against the defendant he would use the steno's notes for an appeal.

"All right," the judge said, "granted." His own glance at the stenographer telegraphed to all assembled that he had not just fallen off the turnip truck.

While Bomber huddled with Melissa, I went off to Cornwell Street and the office of Foster Teague, attorney-at-law, to retrieve the list of contributors to Easy Noggle's third trust deed.

"You know, kid," Foster Teague said, standing imperiously at the door to his private office with a document copy in his hand, "I thought I was doing Easy a favor. If I had any idea this kind of heavy drama would result, I wouldn't have touched the transaction with a ten foot pole."

I nodded as though I understood and agreed. Secretly, however, I was wondering why he was trying to justify himself to me. Convincing Bomber and the jury might have served his cause better. Now that I understood his place in the loan scheme—how it was really a nice money-making scheme for him at no financial risk to himself—it took the edge off his professed altruism. Teague was doing Easy a favor similar to the many favors Easy would have had us believe he was doing for so many others.

Teague swished the document at me not unlike a matador teasing a bull with his cape. "There it is. Read it and weep. I've never been so anxious for anything to be over in my life as I am for this—a real nightmare," he said, and he turned on his heel and took a step back into his office. He shut the door with a little more force than I thought necessary.

I wanted to ask him about all the inconsistencies he had uttered at the trial, but I decided it would not profit either of us. Anything he said to me here could be denied in court, and that was the only place it would count. In the comfort and safety of my car, I looked at the list.

Foster Teague had not been a happy camper since being required by the court to turn over the list. I had remained suspicious that he might alter the list for some reason, like if he had a lot of heavy organized crime figures on it. The surprise I got was not what I expected. Instead, buried among a passel of unfamiliar names with shares of the loan in 20,000 dollar increments, was our own Melissa McHagarty for two shares, or 40,000 clams. Alas, she had been outdone by Lavinia Virgil, Easy's perennial girlfriend, who was listed at 60,000 dollars.

When I returned to the court conference room with the document, Bomber had broken for lunch. Melissa was being led out by the matron to go to the bathroom then have lunch in the holding tank. The indignity of it all to this most dignified of women tore at my heart.

"Well, me boy," Bomber greeted me in an expansive mood that signaled his session with Melissa had gone well. "What did you find?"

I feared what I found would dumbfound Bomber and sink his mood. Some implosion of the curmudgeon would not surprise me.

Rather than suffer the spittle that was bound to accompany any explanation I could give, I handed him the document with the list of names of the lenders on the third trust deed on Easy's house.

I watched his eyes travel down the page. I tried to gauge the time and reaction to his spying the familiar name, and I wasn't off by more than a second.

But instead of the explosion I expected, he just said, "Well, well, well. Will you look at that?"

He dropped the list on the table in front of him and put his hand to his neck and pushed the skin back in that patented gesture that seemed to be calculated to smooth out impending wrinkles.

"You know, I don't believe I've ever been so glad to see a case come to its conclusion. I almost said ending, but I fear that is too optimistic."

"Appeal?" I asked.

"I don't think so. I don't think this judge has screwed

anything up. No, I am just wondering what surprises we will get even after the case is decided. And how long it will be until we see the last of them?"

"What are you going to d-do..." I said, pointing to the document on the table, "with that?"

His hand massaged his neck again.

"I haven't decided," he said. "My first inkling is of course to walk off the case. This is *your* baby, and you could step in or not."

There it was—my worst fear.

"On the other hand, my competitive spirit leads me on to ever greater challenges. This info may actually help us. What doesn't help us is that it is yet another morsel that she did not deem me worthy to have. Why?"

I didn't know why.

"You know, we may go against all the common sense of questioning in court and not prepare for this. Just ask her outright what it means."

"Would you?"

"Surprise her?" he sighed. "Probably not. Too risky." He thought a moment. "On the other hand, maybe risk is just what the doctor ordered."

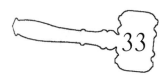

Bomber had Melissa dress in a white suit for her testifying. He wanted to project purity, to make her look as if she were dressed in a surgical gown, ready to save someone's life.

"And remember," he instructed her, "the life you save may be your own."

After she was sworn in, Bomber's early questions put her at ease. Gone was the nervousness I'd discovered in her pre-trial hearing when she was represented by young Kirk Carlisle. Of course, there was no telling if she could maintain her sunny confidence when the district attorney got hold of her for cross-examination.

Her resumé was impressive. In addition to her M.D. from USC Medical School, she had a master's in Public Health from UCLA and a bachelor's degree in Microbiology. She was board certified in her field of General Medicine. She had piled up all kinds of awards: Phi Beta Kappa, Rotary Club Woman of the Year—the same for the local newspaper. Melissa told it all with simple modesty. I could see she was itching to say, 'Oh, that's not as important as it sounds,' but Bomber had surely talked her out of that in advance.

After enough friendly, fuzzy warmth to melt an iceberg, Bomber settled down to the facts he wanted brought out. The contrast between a friendly witness like Melissa and unfriendly ones like Foster Teague and Fingers Sulwip could not have been starker. Bomber was unfailingly courtly and gracious with Melissa, calling her Doctor at every opportunity, bowing, smiling, cooing even. He stood away from the witness so the jury could concentrate on Melissa and her testimony.

"Now, Doctor, directing your attention to the day your husband died, can you remember how you spent the day?"

"I got up and made breakfast for Easy. He liked a big breakfast—bacon, eggs, bagels, jelly, cream cheese and coffee."

"Do you remember what you talked about?"

"He was agitated because I'd refused to continue to make drug purchases to earn large amounts of cash to pay his debts. He said we were about to lose the house if I didn't do something."

"What did you say?"

"I said I'd done it once for him and my conscience was so tormented I couldn't continue."

"How did he respond?"

"By throwing his plate of bacon and eggs at me."

"Did he hit you?"

"Yes."

"Where?"

"My neck, shoulder and breast."

"What did he say?"

"If I wasn't going to be a wife to him and help him when he needed it, he'd have to have me taken care of."

"Those were his exact words? 'Taken care of?'"

"Yes."

"How did you interpret them?"

"I thought he was going to pursue having me killed."

"You say, 'pursue' having you killed—you mean your husband had mentioned the possibility of killing you before?"

"He didn't tell me. I found out."

"How did you find out your husband was planning to kill you?"

"Foster Teague told me he'd heard a rumor Fingers Sulwip had been approached by Easy, my husband, to make the hit."

"Hit? On you?"

"Yes."

"What is your understanding of the word, 'hit' in that context?"

"Kill, murder, assassinate."

"What did you do?"

"I contacted Fingers Sulwip. Set up a meeting."

"Weren't you afraid?"

"I was scared to death."

"So why did you meet him?"

"I couldn't live my life looking over my shoulder every minute. I had to face him—get the truth."

"Where did you meet Fingers Sulwip?"

"In Foster Teague's office."

"Was Mister Teague there?"

"Yes, but in another room."

"So you met with Fingers alone?"

"Henry Ziggenfoos went with me for extra protection."

"Tell the jury what was said at that meeting."

"I told Mister Sulwip I'd heard he had been hired to kill me. He denied it, but in such a way that made me believe it was true. I asked how much he had been offered to do the job. He said he hadn't been offered anything, then added that a job like that from a professional would probably run about twenty thousand."

"Twenty thousand to kill a woman?" Bomber asked, his tone of outrage.

"Yes," she said. "I asked the same thing. He said man, woman, a target's a target. I believe he called it a snuff job. Then I asked how much it would take to get him *not* to *snuff* me. He said there was a lot more to it than money. 'What?' I asked. He said things like honor, reputation, ethics."

"Ethics? He said hit men have a sense of ethics?"

"Yes."

"What did he mean?"

"Objection."

"Oh, okay, did he *say* what he meant by a sense of ethics?"

"He said a man who dealt in hits or snuffs did not auction his skill to the highest bidder. First of all, there was the secrecy requirement. It wouldn't do to have people *know* about the arrangements. Then if someone did, going back and forth to get the most money was unethical, he said."

"Did he happen to comment on the ethics of murder for hire?"

"That didn't seem to bother him."

"I see. Did you then attempt to hire him to kill the man who you thought had hired him to kill you—your husband?"

"No. I just wanted him to *not* kill me," she said. "It was Foster who suggested I hire someone else to get Easy before he got me. He said if Easy wanted the job done, he could get someone to do it. Not everyone would kill a woman, but eventually he'd find someone hungry enough. Besides, he said, 'In this day of women's liberation and all the noise for equality, there were more *professionals* who were less squeamish about wasting a woman. They want to fight in wars, for God's sakes,' he said."

This testimony, which should have struck our hearts as horrible, struck me instead as absurdly funny, and I had to fight to keep from laughing. The audience was not doing so well. Even Judge Pendegrast had a wry smile on his face.

"How did your meeting with Fingers Sulwip conclude?"

"I told him for all practical purposes Easy was broke and probably couldn't pay him anyway."

"What did he say?"

"I always get half up front."

Now nobody could contain themselves, and the place broke into a unison guffaw—my mind, I'm not proud to say, was not on the horror and degradation of one human being hiring another to kill yet another—or the tawdriness of the financial shenanigans—but bizarrely on how I was going to capture that grand guffaw in my musical piece about the romp. If it had been a suite for orchestra I could have had fun with the percussion section, but a sonata for violin and piano was more restrictive—a duo you might think of as sedate. I could use glissandos on both violin and piano—perhaps going opposite directions simultaneously. But it would be a pale imitation of the real thing.

Judge Pendegrast, who was laughing right along with the rest of us, decided we all needed a break from this levity and called a fifteen minute recess in the hope that when we returned we would be in a better frame of mind to buckle down to the seriousness of the matter.

I could tell Bomber was pleased with Melissa's testimony as he strode back to the defense table with Melissa and a bailiff. The judge came in, directed Melissa to resume the stand, then asked for the jury to be readmitted.

As they came in, Bomber and I watched their faces for signs that they were as impressed with Melissa's testimony as we were. But they were a grim looking bunch, and if there was any sympathy in their hearts, it did not show on their faces. Axel Johnson, I thought, looked especially grim.

When the jury was seated, Judge Pendegrast said, "You may proceed, Mister Hanson."

"Thank you, Your Honor," Bomber said, and stood in his position near the defendant table so the jury once again had a clear view of the doctor and her testimony.

"Now, Doctor," he began, "there has been some talk of a loan on your house, specifically a third trust deed. Can you tell us how the title to the home was taken?"

"Fred Noggle, as his sole and separate property."

"Your name was not on the title?"

"No."

"Why not?"

"I signed a prenuptial agreement agreeing to his retaining all of his property in his name."

"Had you been contributing financially to the cost of building the house?"

"Yes."

"And maintaining it?"

"Yes."

"But you weren't listed on the title?"

"No."

"You quitclaimed your interest to your husband?"

"Yes."

"Why?"

"He wanted it. Easy was devoted to money and the power of money. I was in a different line—my line was helping people. Easy said his comfort level was not acceptable if I was on the title. That was all right with me. Money was just a lot more important to him than to me. He was always talking about his comfort level. That was his test for any issue—how did it sit with his comfort level?"

"And what exactly was his comfort level?"

"Anything he wanted it to be. Always, as far as I could tell, it was what served his interests."

"There came a time, did there, when your husband experienced financial difficulty?"

"Yes," she said, nodding enthusiastically. "*Severe.* He lost everything."

"How did he react to that?"

"He was devastated, angry, surly, churlish. Very hard to live with."

"Does the name Lavinia Virgil mean anything to you?"

She dropped her eyes demurely, a Bomber staple. "Yes. She was Easy's girlfriend."

Bomber looked stunned, another staple. "*Before* your marriage?"

"And during. He never let her go."

"Do you know why he didn't marry her?"

"She knew he already had a wife."

"You?"

"No, another."

"Do you know her name?"

"Ursula York."

"So your husband, Easy Noggle, had not only a girl-friend, but a wife when you married him?"

"Yes."

"When did you find this out?"

"The only time I saw her, she came to my office while Easy and I were together. He told me their divorce was almost final, but Ursula was hysterical on the subject. Still extremely jealous. I didn't find out until after the wedding they never divorced."

"Did you realize having two wives was against the law?"

"Objection."

"Sustained."

"Did you ever discuss the legality of having two wives with your husband after it came to light?"

"Yes."

"What did he say?"

"He said he didn't have any talent for spurning women. She wouldn't give him a divorce, and he didn't have the guts to pursue it alone. It just didn't sit well with his comfort level."

"And the girlfriend. Why didn't he marry *her?*"

"She didn't want to marry him. She was satisfied with the position of girlfriend—the other woman. She just didn't want him under foot all the time. He also said I was known and respected in the community, and he hoped that respect would rub off on him."

"Have you ever talked to either of these women?"

"After the wedding I got a call from the wife to tell me she was still married to him, and if there was ever a consideration of inheritance, she would stake her claim."

"How did you react?"

"I was stunned that my husband was a bigamist, of course. As for her claim on his money, I didn't care. I didn't marry Easy for his money. I made enough on my own."

"Why did you marry him?"

"I loved him," she said as though the answer had to be obvious. Too bad there weren't any noticeable sentimentalists on the jury. "I wanted children. I wasn't getting younger. He was a great boyfriend—solicitous, eager to please, to fulfill my every desire. Courtly."

"Did that change with the marriage?"

"Yes, instantly."

"Do you know why?"

"I think the financial pressures were getting to him. There was all this investigation that I didn't know about—he didn't tell me about those things."

"You say investigations. Was it your understanding there was some illegality involved?"

"I got that idea after things began to appear in the paper."

"What things?"

"About his Ponzi schemes, where he misled people into thinking giving him money assured these extraordinary returns."

"Did he ask you for money?"

"Yes."

"Did you give him any?" Bomber asked.

"I gave him all I had, but that was not enough. He had taken so much and spent so much, he could never get ahead. I guess he was disappointed that I didn't have more."

"Objection, speculative," Web said.

"Sustained."

"I'll rephrase," Bomber said. "Did Easy ever tell you he thought you had more money than you did?"

"Yes. He said that was a disappointment, and his attitude toward me plunged from then on. He became abusive, neglectful. We stopped communicating."

"How did that make you feel?"

"Miserable."

"Did you do anything about it? Communicate your feelings to Easy?"

"I tried, to no avail. Then when he found out he was about to lose his house he came to me on bended knee. I could save him. I alone. I was so encouraged at his new interest, I'd have done anything."

"What did he want you to do?"

"Make large drug buys from my legitimate suppliers. Uppers, downers, morphine."

"Why did he say he wanted you to do that?"

"He said it was all that was left to save not only his house, but him."

"You agreed to do it?"

"No, I resisted. We both knew it was illegal and much as I wanted to help him, I didn't want to go to jail for it."

"But you eventually agreed to make the drug buys?"

"Yes," she said, hanging her head in shame.

"Why did you change your mind?"

"He just wore me down. He picked away at me for two weeks, how I didn't care for him. He told me I was a heartless bitch, I passed myself off as a healer, yet I wouldn't do this simple thing to heal my own husband. Mine and someone else's I thought, but I didn't dare say that aloud to him. He'd have killed me."

"Were you afraid he would kill you?"

"Of course! Constantly, after I'd heard he had hired Fingers Sulwip."

"What was your relationship to Foster Teague?"

"He came to me for some medical attention. We became friendly."

"Lovers?"

"Goodness no. He has a wife, I had a husband, and he was my patient."

"But you were also good friends?"

"We were acquaintances. I must say my esteem for him leaped quantitatively when he told me he knew my husband had tried to have me killed. Because Foster Teague set up the meeting with Fingers Sulwip, he saved my life."

She had tears in her eyes. Good, good, I thought, she is making a stunning witness.

"Did you have any further business relationship with Foster Teague?"

She considered a moment. "Only my small participation in the loan to Easy."

"Loan? You mean the third trust deed on the house?"

"Yes."

"*You* loaned him the money?"

"All I had—wasn't much in the scheme of the loan—forty-thousand dollars, about four percent."

"Did Easy know you had done that?"

"No, I didn't tell him."

"He never mentioned that someone else had told him?"

"No."

"Why didn't *you* tell him? Or just give him the forty thousand?"

"It would have been a drop in the bucket. It would have bought Easy perhaps two to three weeks, and not solved his larger problem with the law. He would have probably resented it at the time. I don't know, I wanted to do something. He told me he was trying to get a loan to complete the house from Foster Teague, so I called to offer my help. It turned out to be what Mister Teague needed to complete the loan."

"Did you expect to be repaid?"

"I don't know what I expected at that point. It wasn't that important to me."

Melissa had come through the surprise question with flying colors. Bomber just beamed his approval.

"Only a few more questions, Doctor. Did you murder your husband, Easy?"

"No."

"Did you ever think about doing it?"

She frowned. "I'm a doctor. Doctors *save* lives, they don't take them, no matter what the provocation."

"What was the greatest provocation to killing your husband?"

"When I refused to make a second drug buy to prop Easy up, he became vicious. It was mostly mental anguish, but, as I said he abused me physically also—though his kicks and punches never landed on my face. I suspect he knew if I was visibly damaged his game would be up."

"Objection," Web said. "Speculative, unresponsive."

"Oh, I think it will do. Overruled."

"Did you give Easy—Fred Noggle the injection that killed him?"

"I don't know. I gave him an injection, but I don't know if someone gave him another. I was giving him weekly injections—vitamins and testosterone. I had put the vitamin B12 in the syringe, then I became distracted. Someone came to the door to proselytize me for their religion. Then the phone rang. Then I forgot."

"How long was it between when you filled the syringe with the vitamins and your giving him the shot?"

"I don't remember exactly."

"Best guess?"

"Several hours."

"Was there anyone else in the house in those hours?"

"I don't know. I don't remember anything unusual, but people could be in that cavernous house without anyone knowing it."

"When did you finally remember to give Easy his vitamin shot?"

"When he yelled at me, 'Melissa! Where's my shot?'"

"Then you did what?"

"Went into the kitchen. I had been in the bedroom on the first floor. The kitchen was on the second. I went up, found the syringe where I had left it in the kitchen, took it into the living room where Easy was, gave him the shot, and returned to the bedroom. When I returned to make dinner, I saw Easy slumped in his chair. When he did not answer me I checked and found him dead. I called nine-one-one immediately."

"What was your reaction?"

"Shock."

"Did you at any time wipe your fingerprints off the syringe?"

"No."

"Thank you, Doctor McHagarty. No further questions."

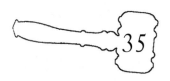

It was the district attorney's turn to question Melissa. He would not be as friendly.

Web stood with a grimace he must have fancied disarming. Melissa smiled back as though she were taken in.

The district attorney started with a bang. "Now, Miss McHagarty," (he was not about to elevate her status in the eyes of the jury by calling her doctor), "when did you first decide to kill your husband?"

"I never decided to kill my husband."

Bomber could have objected, but she did so well on her own.

"Did you really believe he would have you killed?"

"Of course I believed it," she said, and hurriedly added, "His first wife died mysteriously. I think he killed her."

"I object!" Web exploded, then caught himself using the wrong terminology. "I didn't ask that question. I move her answer be stricken from the record as unresponsive, inflammatory, prejudicial. I ask the court to instruct the jury to disregard that editorial, gratuitous contribution."

Judge Pendegrast stared at Web, waiting for him to run down. When the music stopped, Judge Pendegrast asked, "Are you finished?"

"Yes, Your Honor."

"So moved. The jury shall disregard the part of Doctor McHagarty's answer referring to the death of Mister Noggle's first wife."

Fat chance, I thought.

"Your honor," Web said, "might I respectfully request the stenographer read back the last question and answer as amended?"

Judge Pendegrast nodded, "The court reporter will read the last question and answer—as amended."

The reporter picked up the paper tape, similar to an old adding machine tape and looked for the proper place. Reporter: "The district attorney: 'Did you really believe he would have you killed?' Witness: 'Of course I believed it.'"

"Thank you," Web said quickly, to cut off the rest of the answer in case the court reporter didn't get it.

I snuck a look at the jury. I was pretty sure the rest of the answer was playing in their minds.

"All right, Miss McHagarty, weren't you by then his sole source of income?"

"I don't know what other income he may have had. Easy was secretive about his finances. At any rate, my income didn't come anywhere near satisfying his needs. What would have satisfied him was if I had continued to buy the drugs he sold to keep his head above water."

"And did you buy the drugs?"

"Once. But I refused to continue."

"And why was that?'

"My conscience finally got the best of me."

"You knew you could go to jail for it?"

"Yes."

"Why do it even once if you knew it was illegal?"

She slumped a bit, acknowledging Web's point.

"It was stupid. I did it for my husband," she said, the sadness thickening her voice. "I had no need for the money or the big house. That was Easy's baby. Easy was so desperate."

"What do you mean?"

"His troubles with the law—his illegal investment schemes."

"And you added an illegality of your own to the mix?"

Melissa said nothing.

"Isn't that correct?"

"Yes," she answered softly.

"And when you killed him you knew it was illegal?"

"I didn't kill him."

Bomber stood. "Your Honor, I would respectfully request you remind the prosecutor of the rules of evidence, which he knows full well but seems to be flaunting, perhaps out of desperation."

"That was uncalled for," Web said.

"And so is your examining in the form of questions. You're suggesting things not in evidence. It is highly prejudicial."

"All right, gentlemen," Judge Pendegrast said. "Please confine your questions to facts in evidence. And Mister Hanson, you know you can cut the frills with me."

"Yes, Your Honor. I stand corrected."

"All right, Miss McHagarty—"

"Oh, and that's another thing," Bomber said. "Melissa McHagarty is a medical doctor. Respect for that achievement as well as social convention and just good manners dictate he should use that title. The prosecutor took umbrage when I called Fingers Sulwip 'Fingers'. He insisted I call him *Mister* Sulwip. This is no different unless you find, as I do, that the doctor is more entitled to her title than a convicted felon is entitled to be called Mister rather than his criminal nickname."

"When this is over your doctor will be a convicted felon," Web blurted.

"Oh my God!" Bomber said striking his palm on his forehead. "That is *so* out of order."

"All right," Judge Pendegrast was angry, "that's enough. That was uncalled for Mister Grainger. The jury will disregard the prosecutor's characterizations of the witness, and it will be stricken from the record. Now get hold of yourselves, gentlemen. And call her Doctor, Mister Grainger!"

Bomber sat back down, a little smug in his victory. Actually, he was just calling attention to Web's excesses. Secretly he loved for the district attorney to go too far in the hope of offending a few jurors who would take their offense into the jury room for their deliberations.

"All right, Doctor," Web said putting just a skosh too much emphasis on the title, "you have a license to practice medicine?"

"Yes."

"Is it current?"

"Yes."

"You keep up with current practices, ethical as well as scientific?"

"Yes."

"How do you keep up?"

"Reading. Taking courses. We are required to take so many courses to keep abreast of new developments in the field."

"And you do that?"

"Yes."

"Is the practice of filling a syringe, then leaving it for some time before injecting it into a patient a normal procedure?"

"No, it is not."

"But that is what you did on the day your husband died?"

"Yes."

"Was that a normal practice of yours?"

"No."

"Would you do that in the hospital?"

"No."

"Or in your office?"

"No."

"There, I believe you would withdraw the substance to be injected from the vial immediately before giving the shot, correct?"

"Yes."

"That is the accepted, proper, ethical and professional medical practice?"

"Yes."

"Had you done that before at home, with injections intended for your husband? Filled the syringe and let it sit, walked away from it, come back to give it to him?"

"I may have."

"Why do you say that?"

"I had only vitamin B-12 and testosterone, and I wasn't afraid anyone else would substitute anything else."

"But you also had the cyanide, didn't you? The records showed you bought the poison. Couldn't you have switched the vitamins for the poison?"

"No."

"Did anyone else know you had it?"

"I don't know."

"How about the drug salesman, Henry Ziggenfoos," Web asked. "He knew you had the poison?"

"I don't know," she said.

"You *did* buy the poison?"

"Yes."

"From whom?"

"Henry Ziggenfoos' company."

"Henry Ziggenfoos was your representative. Your salesman?"

"Yes."

"So you bought the poison," Web said. "You had the syringe?"

"Yes, but I didn't give him the poison."

"But you gave him the shot?"

"Yes."

"And he died?"

"Yes."

"Of that poison?"

"That was what the coroner said."

"You doubt it?"

"I have no personal knowledge."

The questioning was getting rougher, and Melissa was keeping her cool. I was proud of her. She was not telling an easy story to believe, Web was pounding away, and yet she seemed credible. At least she was creating some doubt.

"And why did you buy that poison?"

"For self-protection."

"Against what?"

"Easy killing me."

"Why not a gun?"

"I don't handle guns. I wouldn't know what to do with one."

"You did know what to do with a syringe?"

"Yes."

"And so you put the poison in it, shot him with the cyanide and killed him?"

"No."

"Doctor McHagarty," Web's tone subsided, "if you were so afraid of your husband, why didn't you just leave?"

"I thought of it, of course. I even talked to him about it, but he went ballistic, said he'd kill me if I left."

"And you believed him?"

"Oh, yes."

"That he was being literal?"

"Yes."

"Now, you say the poison was for self defense, correct?"

"Yes."

"Can you tell the jury how that would work? I mean, suppose he came at you with a gun or a knife, or he tried to strangle you, how would you get to the syringe in time to protect yourself?"

"That's an excellent point, Mister Grainger, and after the heat of my irrational passion cooled, I finally realized that."

"You didn't keep a syringe loaded and handy, just in case?"

"No. I thought about it, but realized I would be no physical match for Easy. He could very easily overpower me. And if he succeeded in hiring an assassin, I would be dead without ever hearing the sound of the gun."

Her answer seemed to surprise Web, and he paused, reflecting a few beats too long.

"All right, Doctor. Is it fair to say you fell out of love with your husband, Easy Noggle?"

"I don't think I have the answer to that mystery. I cared for him to the end. Disenchanted perhaps. Out of love? Probably not."

"Come now, with all he put you through, you came to hate him, did you not?"

"Hate? No—definitely not."

"You killed him, didn't you?"

"No."

"That is certainly not a loving act."

"Objection," Bomber said.

"Sustained. Just ask questions, Mister Grainger."

"You bought the poison?"

"Yes."

"You filled the syringe?"

"Not with the poison."

"I didn't ask you that. You filled the syringe?"

"Every week, yes."

"On the day your husband died, you filled the syringe?"

"Yes, but not with the poison."

"With something?"

"Yes, vitamin B12."

"And you injected him?"

"Yes."

"And he died?"

"Yes."

"No further questions."

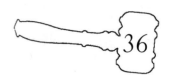

It was time for the character witnesses. There is a difference of opinion about character witnesses. Some think they help, some think they're a waste of time. If a guy is caught holding up a liquor store at gunpoint and a minister comes to court to say deep down he is a good soul—good but troubled—does anyone vote to acquit?

In this case, Bomber thought Melissa's character was the best thing we had going for us. And I lined up no less than 168 of the 186 who were on the doctor's list.

Of course, we had no illusions that the judge would sit still for all those witnesses attesting to Melissa's good character. But Bomber would milk it for all it was worth.

"Any more witnesses, Mister Hanson?"

"Yes, Your Honor, I have a list of one hundred sixty-eight witnesses who are most eager to testify under oath about the defendant's sterling character. We realize this may be taxing on the court's time, but..."

Web interrupted. "Your Honor, may I approach the bench?"

"Yes," the judge said, "good idea."

Web began at the bench. "Just when you think Bomber has exhausted his tricks, he pulls from his sleeve one hundred sixty-seven character witnesses..."

"One hundred sixty-eight," Bomber corrected him.

"...that he wants to put on the stand," Web continued. "He wouldn't only put the jury to sleep, he'd kill them. We'd have a mistrial and have to start over."

"Web!" Bomber said, too loudly, "that's absolute poetry! I didn't know you had it in you."

Judge Pendegrast smiled and frowned at the same time, giving the smile a rather pained quality.

"I'm sure Bomber doesn't intend to put all one hundred sixty-nine of them on the stand."

"There are only one hundred sixty-eight."

"Surely you don't intend...?"

"And why not?" Bomber asked rhetorically. "My client is accused of a capital crime she is incapable of committing as the preponderant testimony will attest."

"I offer a compromise of three," Web said.

"Three!" Bomber exclaimed. "A psychotic axe-murderer can dig up *three* character witnesses."

"Four then," Web was being generous.

Judge Pendegrast looked at Bomber. "Really, you know we aren't going to devote that much time. The idea can be gotten across with a small percentage. We can acknowledge the total number and say in the interest of time we are only hearing from two percent or so."

"Two percent?! That's *three*!"

"Well, perhaps we can work a compromise. What do you offer, Bomber?"

"Say twenty-five, and read the others into the record as individual stipulations."

The judge raised an eyebrow and turned to Web. "Mister District Attorney?"

"I think three is plenty. You can say he has a lot more but it would be ridiculous to numb the jury like that—not to mention the rest of us."

"I think the prosecutor has already numbed the jury in his favor. I want to wake them up with the sense the community has of the prosecutor's handpicked defendant."

"Oh, Bomber, she was no such thing. The police got her—slam dunk. We have *all* the evidence, and you want to confuse the jury into thinking character witnesses are evidence? Well, they aren't."

"Ever think of teaching torts, Web?"

"All right, gentlemen," Judge Pendegrast said, "enough fun and games. I find both your positions untenable. Do you care to compromise, or shall I rule?"

"You first," Bomber said to Web.

Web pouted. "I suppose I could go to five on the stand with some mention that there were others."

"One hundred sixty-three others."

"Yes, but we don't know that precisely."

"Yes we do," Bomber said, and took from his pocket a list and waved it. The jury was watching but ostensibly couldn't hear, though Bomber did have a real talent for communicating his part of these secret conferences.

Bomber said he thought for his compromise ten would be a huge sacrifice. "Without cross-examination I can put them through in a half a day," he said. "But I think it is vital we read the others into the record as stipulations. I mean the charge here is *murder*, not D.U.I."

"All right, Bomber, I understand your side and yours too, Mister Grainger. We'll hear from six," he said, "and you may have the names of the balance read into the record."

"Your Honor," Web said, "how do we know they are all legitimate?"

Bomber threw up his hands. "Well," he said too loudly, "put them on the stand. You can cross-examine them to your heart's content."

"What's your wish on the matter, Mister District Attorney?" the judge asked.

Web sulked. "Well, at least give us the list. We can make random checks."

"All right with you, Mister Hanson?"

"Fine," he said.

Web held out his hand. Bomber looked at it. "Your Honor, shouldn't we do this in front of the jury, on the record?"

"All right." We returned to our seats and the judge instructed the jury in what was to transpire. Bomber gave the fifty-three pages of names, addresses, phone numbers, occupations and received comments of each of the proposed witnesses. They were liberally spaced to make the stack look bigger than it had to be.

We had one witness standing by, and I was sent out in the hall to telephone the others while the clerk read the names into the record. A lot of them were names familiar to the community—philanthropists, the mayor and city counsel, hospital staff, high-profile patients. Bomber had marked the five he wanted me to call, handed me the list and said, "Use your celery phone." That was what he called cell phones, which he wouldn't touch with a ten foot pole. I think he'd rather climb a telephone pole and hook into a high wire than to use a cell phone. Every time Bomber saw someone on a cell phone he complained about it. "Look at the celery phones," he'd say, "you might as well be talking to a stalk of celery." It was a *non sequitur* I didn't question. "What is it with these people? Afraid of their own company? Have to be in constant communication with an endless stream of small talk? I mean, listen to them sometime. They are shameless about sharing their private lives with strangers. The other day I saw a guy turning a corner in his car while dialing a number on his celery phone."

So I called my list—the mayor first, to give her first choice of times. Then I called the hospital chief of staff, the doctor who had examined her for her Board certification, the most generous local philanthropist, and the head of the medical clinic, where she worked, and where we hoped she would continue.

Everyone was more than eager to oblige.

When I returned to the courtroom the clerk was droning on reading the names into the record. Bomber looked at me, and I gave him a surreptitious thumbs up.

When the clerk finished, Bomber stood and said, "Your Honor, I would respectfully request that the list be given to the jury to take into their deliberation room."

"Yes," Judge Pendegrast said, "it is in evidence."

Web stood. "I would just as respectfully request that instruction be given that the prosecution has not verified any of this. Since it was an eleventh hour introduction, we did not have time."

"So ordered," the judge said. "Your first character witness, Mister Hanson."

"The defense calls Mister Wilton Tankersley."

Wilton was not shy of his biblical allotment of years, but he exuded energy and some grace as he took the stand, put his hand on the Bible offered by the clerk, and swore to tell the truth, the whole truth and nothing but the truth—a phrase I always thought of as being semantic overkill. Truth is, after all, truth. It is not truth and something else, and it is not half truth, but the old timers who made up this court jargon liked to get flowery sometimes.

"Mister Tankersley," Bomber began, "would you tell the jury how it came about that you are appearing here as a character witness for Doctor McHagarty?"

"Well," he said, leaning back on the witness chair, "she's only the finest doctor that ever come down the pike."

"Why is that?"

"Well, I'll tell you. The wife up and developed these migraines—headaches, you know, but real severe headaches. Blinding pain. I takes her in to Doctor McHagarty and she checks her out and diagnoses this tumor right away and sets us up with a surgeon. This is life and death stuff, and Doctor McHagarty doesn't flinch. When the surgeon on the other floor over by the clinic says he can't operate—too risky, and says he doesn't know anybody who can—why Doctor McHagarty just goes to work, calling all over the country until she finds this surgeon in North Carolina who says, 'Let me see the x-rays'. She doesn't FedEx 'em like your garden variety family doctor might do, no, she gets on the plane, goes to North Carolina, sees the doctor herself and shows him the x-rays. Goes over the wife's history, and he says he can do it, and the next thing we know we are on a plane to Raleigh, North Carolina, and who do you think is there to meet the plane?"

"Who?"

"Doctor McHagarty."

I peeked at the jury—those hardest of hearts. I could be wrong, but I thought this was the first inroad Bomber had made.

Wilton Tankersley went on, "And she just stayed there with us through the entire ordeal. She knew how scared we were, going to a strange place like that. The wife had never been out of California, and I wasn't much of a traveler myself—never North Carolina. And seeing Doctor McHagarty there was…I mean, I can't even put it in no words…just the most wonderful thing. I swear we both just broke up when we saw her. This was a *doctor*, after all. She had other patients and appointments she had to cancel." He shook his head. Tears were forming in his eyes.

"Was the operation a success?" That was a question Bomber would not have asked had he not known the answer.

"Oh, yes. It was wonderful—with Doctor McHagarty there reassuring us every step of the way. Lizzie's good as new now—well, not any of us getting younger to be good as new, but she's doing right fine."

"And you felt Doctor McHagarty deserves some of the credit?"

"Well, yes, sure I do. We both do. More credit than the guy who did the carpentry on Lizzie's head. I mean, North Carolina! We'd a never found a doctor in North Carolina. Plus, we'd a been scared to death going to a strange hospital like that. Doctor McHagarty knew that and she…she did…I mean, there's just no telling how grateful we are…not the kind of thing I have the learning to express." Tears began to flow.

Bomber said softly, "You're doing fine," and that was the understatement of the trial.

"Did you make any personal sacrifice to come and testify?"

Wilton Tankersley waved a hand of dismissal at Bomber as though it were of no consequence. "We had a trip planned, is all."

"Where to?"

"Going to do Europe—first time—all the spots: London, Paris, Rome—you name it."

"Have your reservations—plane tickets?"

"Yeah, we did."

"Will you get a refund?"

Wilton Tankersley wrinkled his nose. "No, they wouldn't give us anything."

"You a rich man, Mister Tankersley?"

"Oh, no, but I'll tell you something, fella, wild horses couldn't a kept me from coming here to say my peace about this here wonderful woman. They just don't make 'em like that no more. I don't think they ever did."

"We told you we had one hundred sixty-eight people eager to testify, didn't we?"

"Yeah."

"And you could have gone on your trip?"

He nodded. "You told me. But I told you, 'Lissen here, young fella, I'm going to that court to say my peace about Doctor Melissa McHagarty and nobody gonna stop me. I'll bust down the door if I have to. I'll arm wrestle those sheriffs if I have to, but I'm telling my peace and I don't care if they throw me in jail.'" He looked straight at the defendant. "Melissa McHagarty—we owe you big time."

Melissa was crying, and Bomber returned to stand behind her and rub her shoulders with both hands—just in case anybody missed her tears. "No more questions, Mister Tankersley, and thank you from the bottom of our hearts for coming."

Wisely, Web the prosecutor said, "No questions."

The other character witnesses were just as good, just not as colorful. They emphasized her standing in the medical community—tops—and the community at large. She was one well thought of lady, and I encouraged myself in the belief that the jury was definitely softening.

The defense rested. The judge called a lunch break.

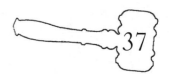

37

The jury speeches were next. Web went first.

"Murder is murder, ladies and gentlemen. If the best person takes the life of the worst, it is still murder. You do not have to be in the difficult position of judging the niceness or worth of the individuals in question. All you have to do is decide if one of them murdered the other.

"In this case, I think you will find the evidence proves murder at the hands of Melissa McHagarty beyond a reasonable doubt.

"Bomber Hanson has endeavored throughout the trial to create doubt in your minds. He is reaching, ladies and gentlemen, and it is painfully obvious."

Web reviewed the evidence, piece by piece, and the evidence as we know, was not favorable to us. "And remember," he said, "you make your deliberations and your verdict based solely on the evidence—*nothing else!*

"She did it, ladies and gentlemen. It's a simple case, inasmuch as any case with Bomber Hanson can be simple, for my learned opponent has a way of obscuring the simple facts and twisting them unrecognizably in favor of his client.

"It began simply, if sinisterly. Doctor McHagarty injected her late husband with poison while he thought he was getting a vitamin shot. What did McHagarty think? First she told us she *didn't* inject him, but that was surely unbelievable. She had been giving him these shots for years. Who else was he going to let inject his buttocks? Finally, she saw the absurdity of that and she changed her story. She *did* plunge that deadly syringe into her *late* husband, *but* she says she thought it was a vitamin shot—someone else must have put the cyanide in the needle. Really?" Web hoisted his eyebrows to show what he thought of that.

"*Who?* And *why?* I assure you, ladies and gentlemen, anything advanced along those lines by the defense attorney will be most fanciful—the stuff of dreams and fantasy.

"And I don't say if you or I were in his shoes, with a hopeless case such as his, why we wouldn't try the same thing. There is an old adage at law: when the facts are against you, shout about the law, when the law is against you, shout about the facts, and when they're both against you, shout like hell."

He got polite titters on that one. Not particularly original—Bomber used it all the time, and with somewhat more flair than Web.

"Well, ladies and gentlemen, no one shouts louder than Bomber, but I'm bound to tell you in this case, he has absolutely nothing to shout about."

Bomber hastily scrawled a note on his yellow legal pad and pushed it toward me.

He's right!

"Ladies and gentlemen of the jury, let me tell you something about syringes in the hands of medical personnel. No one gives an injection with a syringe full of a mystery liquid. A doctor has to verify the material in the vial, then open a sealed new syringe, draw the vitamins—or poison—into it, and then, and only then, inject it into the patient.

"The defendant *admitted* giving her husband the shot, after telling us what a trial it was to be married to Easy Noggle. Well, lots of people have unhappy marriages, ladies and gentlemen, but murder is not the solution. Divorce is easy now. There is no *need* to resort to murder.

"Melissa McHagarty resorted to murder. She is guilty of murder. She must pay the penalty for her murder, no matter how upstanding a member of society she was, no matter how disagreeable the victim, she is a murderess, and in this sacred

215

court of law where you sit in judgment, she must be judged for what she is. It may not be a happy decision for you, but ladies and gentlemen, upon my word, it is your duty to return a verdict of guilty as charged.

"Why? Remember my words in my opening remarks to you—m.o.m.—motive, opportunity, means.

"She had the motive, ladies and gentlemen, there's no denying he was a difficult husband and she couldn't cope with him. Then there is the matter of the million dollar insurance policy. If she is acquitted, she can make a case for collecting it. The opportunity she had in spades: She was there in the house *alone* with him. She had the *trust* of the victim—and I don't care what you think of Easy Noggle, when someone *trusts* you with his life, you have an *obligation* to earn that trust.

"And the final M—she had the means—she had procured poison, she had syringes, she knew how to use them.

"M.o.m.—motive, opportunity, means. Melissa McHagarty had all three—as solidly as any case I've ever tried, ladies and gentlemen. I thank you for your attention—the state and your neighbors will thank you for doing your duty and returning that verdict of 'Guilty as charged!'"

I cased the jury again. They seemed sold. I did not envy Bomber trying to win the hearts and minds of this crowd with the thin gruel he had been dished.

As Web sat down, I turned at the sound of the door opening in the back of the courtroom. There, as the vision of loveliness she was, stood my beloved Joan Harding—a ray of sunshine highlighting her. My heart nearly stopped dead in its tracks. Her trip with the L.A. Philharmonic must have been salubrious, as she looked even better than when she'd left.

The bailiff had saved a seat for her, a courtesy endemic to Angelton and Weller County, something a lot harder to come by in Los Angeles.

I realized after our eyes met that my smile must have been broad and sappy. My insides were mush, and I'm afraid I was not paying strict attention to Bomber's argument, so what I have written here is my memory from my cryptic notes, which I now realize are shorn of their usual hearts and flowers poetry.

As they say, you had to be there.

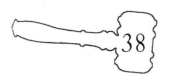

38

"I am always amused and sometimes gratified to hear the prosecutor tell you what I am going to say before I say it," Bomber began, "Sometimes he gives me ideas I wouldn't have had, sometimes he gives me a second opportunity to bolster a point. I find that so often I am out-lawyered by my adversaries, and no one out-lawyers me like our district attorney."

I thought that a clever phrasing of the circumstances. Notice he said no one out-lawyers me *like* the district attorney—not *better* than. I never knew how sharp the jurors were with this sort of chicanery. I suspected that Bomber's reputation was such that most of the people in the courtroom knew he was blowing smoke with his humble pie shtick. A glance at the jury did not disabuse me of that notion.

"Mister Grainger the third would like you to think Doctor McHagarty is evil incarnate—a murderess, no less, one who murders in cold blood. Well, you're intelligent men and women with powers of perception. Look at the doctor sitting here throwing her fate to your hands. If she looks evil to you, if she looks like the cold blooded, premeditated murderess District Attorney Grainger would have you believe she is, I say put her away and toss the key far out in the Pacific. She is *not* the sorceress he paints. You know it, I know it, and I venture to say the prosecutor knows it."

Bomber would call Web the prosecutor again and again. It had a sinister ring to it.

"When the prosecutor built his case against our fair healer, did he stop to consider the character of the woman accused? Did he consider her reputation? Her standing in this community?

"Now, I don't know if you folks have any idea of what it takes to get into a medical school, and that it's even harder to get *out* of one. They don't take or graduate dummies. I wouldn't give a nickel for my chances at it. Law school pales by comparison. So what does the prosecutor suggest in this case? Nothing less than that the defendant was so stupid she, an M.D. no less, murdered her husband in cold blood by lethal injection, knowingly doing it, then incredibly leaving the murder weapon on the dining room table and blithely trundling off to her daily chores of saving people's lives.

"Not only wouldn't a person with that low grade an intelligence not get into medical school, she wouldn't get past kindergarten.

"Well, *who* did it, the prosecutor asks. And *why?*

"It's a good question, but one I submit must be asked and answered by the state. My job is simply to see that the state makes a solid, convincing case beyond a reasonable doubt that my client is guilty. It is not up to me to find the person or persons who substituted that poison for the Vitamin B12 shot.

"Perhaps Easy Noggle would know if we could wake him. What visitors did he have before his bride came back up the stairs of their cavernous castle? Someone he knew, no doubt. What was said? We don't have any idea. Was there an argument? It had to be someone who knew the routine, someone familiar with a syringe, limiting the possible suspects, but not as much as you might suspect. Drug users know syringes, diabetics inject insulin, but it is not my place to investigate crime. I don't have two percent of the resources, staff, computer power and sundry equipment the district attorney's office does. I am a poor solo practitioner, no match for the mighty State of California, which is over thirty million strong.

"Does our case have a weakness? Yes it does. I'll admit that, and the weakness is Melissa bought the poison—and not to kill any rats or vermin. " Bomber stopped short, as though an idea just occurred to him. It was one of his better ploys, this sudden extemporaneous inspiration. "On second thought, based on what we know about Easy Noggle, he may fit the vermin category rather nicely—maybe killing Easy had crossed her mind. Who among us would not have had the same feelings if we had been married to Easy Noggle, a man of consummate ego, obsessed with power and the swindling of his fellows, thrice married without benefit of the divorce laws, a law unto himself? Did the person who finally ended this miserable existence not do mankind a service? That is not for me to say. All I can say is the prosecutor is still a long way from proving his circumstantial case. A circumstantial case is the weakest case. It says look at these circumstances, coincidences really, if we put them all together in a manner pleasing to our side it could be construed as guilt on the part of the defendant.

"Spurious, weak, inappropriate. In this case, inconsequential.

"Now, I've seen a lot of murderers in my time, ladies and gentlemen, most of them I'm frank to tell you, are animals. And I hope that won't hurt the sensibilities of the politically correct among us, but murder takes a certain, and thank goodness an unusual, mindset, which the defendant in this case does not possess. She wanted to do it, she bought the poison, she just didn't have the heart or mind to go through with it. I say one has only to look at this pure good doctor and one cannot fail to see her innate goodness, she lives a life devoted to saving lives, not to taking them.

"I don't know about you, but I wonder at a character as savory as Fingers Sulwip turning away work. If Doctor McHagarty really tried to hire him, why did he turn down the job? He's too fussy? A doctor isn't up to the standards of his clientele? She tried to chisel his price? Look at the two of them, ladies and gentlemen, and decide which of them is telling the truth.

"Take with you to the jury room the personages of Fingers Sulwip and Doctor Melissa McHagarty. Which will you find better company? Which will you deem more trustworthy?

"Now, I'm sure you know all advocates go over their witness's testimony before they appear on the stand. They'd be fools not to. And one of the informal rules is you never ask a question you don't know the answer to. It's too risky.

"Well, I have a confession to make. I did just that. I was as thorough as I could be in consulting with my client, Doctor McHagarty, about her testimony, never telling her what to say. The truth is strong in this case, and it should be strong enough to win the day. But late in the game—and remember I had only a month to prepare this case—a public defender gets more than that. Late in the day my son Tod brought me this document of the million dollar loan made by Foster Teague to Easy Noggle. It had the names of the people who kicked in money for a super risky third trust deed. And lo and behold, there prominent among them was none other than Melissa McHagarty.

"She didn't tell me about this. Forty thousand dollars! It was all she had, she said. She didn't just hand it to Easy as she could have, that would have hurt his pride. So she buried it in a loan. She got no credit for it. It was an anonymous donation out of the goodness of her heart.

"All I had to go on was her name on that document Foster Teague supplied us. So I asked her cold on the stand about it. She could have blushed, she could have faltered. Did she exhibit any sign of chagrin or guilt?

"She did not! You saw her. This is as pure a gesture as I can imagine. And she told it as though it were a footnote on one of her medical reports. She had forgotten about it.

"A woman who loans a man forty thousand dollars to keep his house, all she has—she's not on the title, remember, it's *his* house, not hers—is not a woman who is going to murder that same man.

"How many of us have not been so angry or scared that we haven't had thoughts of murder in our hearts? How many of us murder?

"Doctor McHagarty was *scared*, and I can't blame her. If you can, you have harder hearts than I. How many of us can empathize with someone who has a contract on her head?

"Scary!

"Do you skulk around, watching your back, sleeping with a pistol under your pillow? What good that would do, I never understood. If someone wants to kill you, they aren't going to wait till you wake up and reach for your gun.

"We don't know, and we may never know, how many trips Foster Teague made to the murder scene and in what kind of misleading car. We may never know unless Mister Teague should be indicted by the district attorney for the murder of Easy Noggle."

Web stood as though unsure of himself. "Your Honor, may we strike that from the record? Bomber knows there is no indication of that in the testimony, much as he'd like there to be."

"Fair comment," Bomber offered.

Judge Pendegrast said, "Well, he said it, the jury heard it. I give a lot of leeway in argument. I'll let it stand."

"May I resume, Your Honor?" Bomber said with too high a note of triumph in his voice.

"You may."

"Thank you.

"Now, the 'misunderstanding' about the car service. Why is this important? Because if you wanted to go someplace and not have your car identified, especially if it were a one hundred twenty-five thousand dollar Mercedes Benz, you might go instead in a more nondescript vehicle, as the one Foster Teague used for his visits to the Noggle residence. Why was he there? On one occasion, he says it was to inventory personal property to recoup some of his losses. However, he did admit he had no financial stake in that particular loan. The other occasion he denies being there, in the same car. You decide, ladies and gentlemen. He knew about injections from the Navy. Someone filled that syringe with poison, and it wasn't the defendant.

"Yes, Avery Knapp, the policeman, said Doctor McHagarty claimed not to have given him the injections at the time of the crime. But when you heard from her, she said she gave him an injection—only of vitamins. Someone else, she thought, had given him the lethal injection.

"Sometimes I think the authors of the law on reasonable doubt did you jurors no favors. What were they trying to achieve? I think they were bolstering the presumption of innocence that demands you consider Doctor Melissa McHagarty and defendants like her who stand in front of you, awaiting your powerful judgment, *innocent*—not guilty, unless you are *fairly certain* she is guilty. Your judgment of any defendant's guilt must be *beyond* a reasonable doubt. That's the way we do things in this country, which I am not at all ashamed to say is still far and away the greatest nation on earth, perhaps the greatest nation the world has ever seen. Why so great? Because we treat our fellow citizens with respect, with gratitude in cases of those who have lived for others, as Doctor Melissa McHagarty has.

"We are summoned to this sacred duty of passing judgment on one accused of the heinous crime of murder and, ladies and gentlemen, I cannot for the life of me think of a more critical judgment that you could make in your lifetime. Shall Doctor Melissa McHagarty be returned to the citizenry of this great city that she has so richly served for so many years, or shall she be unceremoniously turned out of our lives to rot in the penitentiary? It's up to you. Her life is in your hands. The law acknowledges the vital importance of your decision. That's why you are asked to be *reasonably certain* that this unspeakable act was executed by Doctor McHagarty, and not by one of the battalions of enemies Easy Noggle had in this state."

Our favorite juror Axel Johnson still had that sour, hang-'em-from-the-apple-tree look on his face.

"It seems almost bizarre to me that the docket for this trial should read the State of California versus Melissa McHagarty when the victim, Easy Noggle, was the enemy of practically everyone in the State of California."

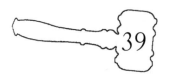

39

"Oh my, but Bomber is at it again, waving the flags of character and reputation," the D.A. rebutted. "But this isn't a libel trial or a slander trial where those qualities are at issue. This is a *murder* trial. If you want to believe this murderer has a heart of gold, that's your prerogative. But what you must believe based on the overwhelming evidence is that, sad as it may be, she *is* a murderess, and we don't take kindly to killers in Weller County, no matter how upstanding they may be in other walks of life.

"Doctors are healers. It is a noble profession. You won't get me to say otherwise, but believe it or not Melissa McHagarty is not the first doctor to be accused and *convicted* of murder. You have a duty to your fellow citizens to punish killers, no matter how they are wrapped; no matter what their *past* good deeds were.

"What would Bomber ask of us? That we acquit anyone with a college education? Anyone who has ever given to charity in their lives? *Good* people? Good people can do bad things, and when they do, ladies and gentlemen, it is *not* our duty to pat them on the head and say, 'Oh, you murdered someone but otherwise you're a good person, so we'll let you go this time.'

"Think of it, we could revolutionize the justice system. We could have a division that separates the good people from the bad, beginning with parking tickets and going right up to murder. We could save a lot of time and trouble just not prosecuting those deemed 'the good.'

Web shook his head. "Ridiculous. You know it, I know it, and Bomber knows it.

"And oh, by the way, Bomber keeps calling me the *prosecutor*, as though I were some sinister force in the society. I'm not, ladies and gentlemen, I'm just a public servant doing my level best to see that murderers and other miscreants pay their debts to society. And I do this without fear or favor to those who are highly educated and those who have many stars in their crowns from good deeds.

"Now, in order to prejudice your thought, Bomber has said Melissa McHagarty devoted her life to saving lives. Not to detract from her profession, her non-specialty, general medicine, seldom if ever entailed the saving of a life. No, a general practitioner is occupied making people feel better. If they are anywhere near death she refers them to some specialist. I only mention this seemingly small point to keep you on your guard against Bomber's exaggerations. He has painted his client as Joan of Arc, Florence Nightingale and Mother Theresa, all rolled into one.

"But, ladies and gentlemen, if any of *them* had committed murder, I would be bound by my oath to prosecute them too.

"I join the defense attorney for praising his client for the good she has done the community. But by the same token, when she murders, society *must* extract justice. We can no more in good conscience let a good person who is guilty off scot-free than we can a bad one. Fortunately, the goodness or badness of this defendant is something outside the responsibility you have for consideration. From that aspect, the law has made it easy for you—just judge on the *facts*. Just judge on this single act of murder. You may want to award the defendant the family doctor of the year award, and I suppose a lot of evidence supporting that fanciful contention has been presented here, but it is ephemera, whitewash, smokescreen. It may do many things, but what it doesn't do is demonstrate in any factual way that Melissa McHagarty is not guilty of the murder of her husband.

"Don't be fooled. If she is Joan of Arc, Florence Nightingale, Sister Theresa all rolled into one, *and* she committed this heinous murder, you *must* return a verdict of guilty as charged. I will concede the defendant was a respected, even beloved member of our community, in exchange for your conceding that we have proven the case against her beyond a reasonable doubt. Murder is murder. Even when the killer can be shown to be better than the victim. And that's what makes this country great. Doing your duty without fear, without favor. Return with a verdict of guilty as charged!"

Though I hated to admit it, I think our fearless district attorney was getting better at jury schmoozing.

There was a recess before the judge would bore everyone to tears with his jury charge: points of law, the framers of trial procedure that would be helpful to the jury. Helpful, perhaps, if you could get them to listen. By the time the judge wrapped up the case with his take on how the intelligent, informed decision should be arrived at, the jurors were glassy-eyed and impatient. Any expectation they would listen to and absorb those monotone renderings of prosecution, defense, and the judge's own canned offerings from dry-as-old-toast law books was highly optimistic.

As soon as the gavel announced the adjournment, I slipped the envelope with my possible scenarios for the murder across the desk to Bomber. He glanced at it.

"What's this?" he asked.

"The s-scenarios you asked f-for."

"Oh, yes, good," he said, and put them in his inside jacket pocket. Then I rushed back to the audience, where Joan and I happily embraced with as much gusto as we thought courthouse decorum would allow.

As we released, Bomber came by and put his moves on Joan, who was his favorite of all my girlfriends (mine too). If his efforts at flirty small talk had not been so cute for a guy his age, they would have been embarrassing.

"Why don't you take a break?" he said to me, "you certainly don't need to sit through another jury charge. I wish I didn't have to." He looked at Joan, "I'm sure you can find more enjoyable ways to pass the time," and then, yes, I kid you not,

Bomber winked at Joan. Though I wanted to crawl through the floor, she took it in good grace with a smile I would say was just right—not so broad Bomber would think he had really scored, and not so thin as to appear insouciant.

"That would be very nice," she said. "You did great, Bomber. I *love* to hear you talk to the jury."

I think she must have heard more than I did.

"I'll call you when we have a verdict," Bomber said, "if you want to be here for it. You don't really have to."

I didn't answer right away. If we won, I wanted to be there. If we lost, what with my nagging Bomber to take the case, and my feelings for our client—I thought I'd rather not.

I nodded tentatively. Joan sensed Bomber might have been disappointed with my notable lack of enthusiasm, so she brightened and said, "Of course we want to be there for the verdict. We wouldn't miss it for the world."

It was like a strong pat on the back to Bomber. He smiled a smile that put me in mind of the grill on his Bentley. "Good! I'll call you." He paused a moment, then said, "And thanks for the scenarios," and patted his breast.

Then he moved away into the hallway, where we heard him telling the press and the TV lovelies, "No predictions," with his hand up as if to stop traffic. "Never know what a jury is going to do."

40

Joan and I retreated to my place, where we made all kinds of music together. Waiting for a verdict is usually the hardest part of a trial for me. This one was harder because I thought we were going to lose it.

When I told Joan my thoughts, she said, "You don't give your dad and his powers of persuasion enough credit. I predict victory. I was much more swayed by Bomber's argument than by the district attorney's."

"But nice as that is," I said, "you weren't at the trial. The evidence is not defendant friendly."

"Well, I don't think she could murder. I know that isn't a very rational approach to the mores of legal persuasion, but it is a strong feeling in my gut."

I put my hand on her middle to see if I could feel anything other than skin that was as soft as satin. I couldn't but I was happy at her optimism. There is nothing that lifts the spirits from the doldrums of pessimism like an optimistic sprite.

In spite of the fact Joan had to be worn out from making music with the Philharmonic, she wanted to read through my *Easy Sonata* for violin and piano. My modesty in producing it for her was overwhelming, but we played it, and she was ebullient in her enthusiasm and praise.

"Tell me about the trial," she said. "I want to understand how it fits the music."

I recounted the testimony as best I could, trying not to be too tedious with details. When I finished, she went to the heart. "What's with this Forest fellow? How do you size him up?"

"Foster Teague. An enigma."

"Think he might have been involved in the demise of the quaintly named Easy?"

"That's a question I have pondered a bit. Bomber would like to have the jury believe that without any hard evidence."

"Why would Teague lie about the car?"

"That's a good question. People don't usually lie if they have nothing to hide. Maybe he was protecting someone?"

"The doctor?"

"Maybe."

"Why?"

"Don't know. According to the testimony they were only acquaintances. He went to her for medical help, but only once, according to him. She credits him with saving her life by telling her of the contract for Fingers to off her."

"Which he denies," she said. "How did that play?"

"Not too convincingly. Fingers is not a pillar of the genteel community. His relationship to Foster Teague is one of the stranger mysteries of the piece." I fiddled with the section I'd written to denote that disjointed harmony. It was as though the piano were playing a different piece than the violin, sort of like a Charles Ives work.

"I see," Joan said, "it doesn't fit together like your normal logic—a lawyer and a crook."

"And it's not so much that you can't have that combo in any family, I mean, they aren't brothers or anything, just married two sisters, but why then do they have this apparent association? Borrowing his car, checking out the house, loaning money on the house of a guy who hired, or tried to, his brother-in-law to hit the doctor. And how did Foster Teague hear about the hit? Did Easy tell him, or Fingers, or neither?"

"Or both?"

"Could be."

"Then why did Melissa invest with Foster Teague if she

barely knew him?"

"Good question. It would seem odd that a man who was raising money for a mortgage on a home would think of asking the man's wife to join in."

"Yeah, you'd think she'd just give it directly and not expect to make a thousand percent interest on it."

"Only forty percent the first year, twenty percent after that."

"Not too bad when banks are paying less than one percent."

"Ah, but Mister Teague cites the risk, and there's no arguing that the way it turned out."

Just then the phone rang. It was airhead Bonnie with the news that the jury had reached a decision. "So hie your cute little buns in the direction of the courthouse, Sweet Meat." Fortunately she broke the connection so no response was necessary. Joan got to see my blushing cheeks.

"It's the jury?"

I nodded. Without another word we hustled out the door and into Joan's car. She drove. When we were underway she asked, "What were these scenarios Bomber spoke of?"

"Oh, he wanted me to write up what I thought could have happened and give it to him at the end of the trial, so he could compare my thoughts, or fantasies, really, with what we found out."

"What *did* you find out?"

"That's just it. We haven't really found out anything."

"What were the scenarios?"

"Well, I was at a loss, so I was completely reaching. One was Easy switched the stuff himself. He wanted to be out of the fray. His life of riches had come crashing down around him and his comfort level, as he liked to call it, must have zeroed out. But powerless as he was then—and I'm convinced he couldn't live without power over his fellow humans—he didn't want to let go altogether. So his final power stroke was to put his wife through this hell. He didn't know she had put all she had into the fund to loan him money for his house. The house she wasn't on the title of. All he knew was she refused to make illegal drug buys to save him, so he solved two problems with one act: Suicide, to look like she murdered him. That way she couldn't collect on the insurance."

"Hm," Joan said, "believe it?"

"I guess not. Of all the problems and antisocial behavior Easy had, I don't think a lack of self-esteem was among them. He was the kind of guy who thought he never made a mistake in his life. He was always right, everyone else was wrong."

"What were your other scenarios?"

"I had one where Henry Ziggenfoos, the drug sales-man, acting the knight in shining armor to protect his heroine, his favorite doctor and customer, did the switch, but was unable to fess up and spend his life's residue in the slammer. Maybe they even had an affair."

"What do you think of that one?" Joan asked.

"Not too much. He didn't come to the trial except once to testify. Though if they were having an affair that might have been a smart move. But I don't get the right vibes about it. Remember, Bomber was pressing me for this and I didn't have a lot of time."

"Anything else?"

"Of course I wanted to fit Foster Teague in there some-where, but I don't peg him for a killer. He had no financial stake in the loan. The house wasn't worth all Easy had against it. He'd had very little contact with Melissa as far as we know. He did keep showing up at the house incognito, I just don't know if he was telling the truth. He lied about his car repair, a seemingly insignificant act, but you know the dictum at law—*falsus in unum, falsus in omnibus.*"

"False in one, false in all?"

"Yes. If you catch someone in a lie, you can assume everything he says is a lie."

"Could they have been lovers?"

"Melissa and Foster?" I was surprised. "He's old

enough to be her father."

"It *has* happened."

"I don't see any chemistry there. I'd say that was a long shot."

"Well, you're getting it over with, why do you look so sad?"

"Because typically a quick verdict favors the prosecution, Joan. It's been what? Three hours? If they are going to acquit they usually deliberate longer. It's not so cut and dry."

Inside the courthouse, the mood at our table was gloomy. Bomber was given to heavy sighing as we waited for the judge and the jury to file in. "Too quick," he muttered in his for-our-ears-only whisper. "I don't like it."

No, I supposed not—no one liked to lose, but I don't know anyone it was harder on than Bomber. Trials were not just a job with Bomber, they were his life. He lived and breathed every one of them. Over time I had become more bold in my recommendations, which cases he should take, which he should not. Though I sometimes thought negative persuasion was a better bet—backing a case in the guise of talking him out of it. This time he'd gone all out for the doctor based solely on my take on her character.

My gut feeling about the outcomes was the opposite of Joan's, and I'd had a lot more experience with juries. Bomber had still more, and he didn't like the portents, so I was preparing my meaningless platitudes: we had horrible luck with the jury, no human being should be expected to mount a murder defense in a month, and Bomber's willingness to do so bespoke a larger than life character. He had done his best in that scant time, bla, bla, bla.

Another wives' tale about juries is that when they march in after the verdict they will look at the winner.

Doesn't happen. It is as though all jurors have heard that canard and fight to do the opposite: stare straight ahead and look at nobody. That's just what this collection of sourpusses did.

I looked at our client, Melissa McHagarty. She looked more nervous than she had on that day of her preliminary hearing a short while ago. My heart went out to her, but seeing her like that did nothing for my sagging spirits.

When the judge asked if they had reached a verdict, and the foreman said they had, I noticed Bomber's hand slip surreptitiously over to squeeze Melissa's arm. She gave a little flinch of surprise, then smiled as though that were the expected result of a preplanned signal.

The sealed verdict was passed by the bailiff to the judge, who opened it; deadpan was de rigueur here, though I thought I noticed a flicker on his face. It wasn't much—a twitch of the lips, a stronger blink of his eye. I was encouraged, then I realized it could mean anything. The verdict was passed to the clerk to read aloud.

He opened the envelope again, and I think these were the slowest seconds I ever saw pass. Our clerk seemed to want to heighten the suspense with pregnant pauses and hapless hesitations.

"We...the jury...find...the defendant...Doctor Melissa McHagarty...not guilty."

The defendant table didn't erupt in delight, but leaned forward as one as if to make sure we had heard correctly. Then, as we seemed to be satisfied the word *not* was in there somewhere, we still didn't jump up and hug and slap on the backs. No high fives for us—we were too stunned.

We sat immobile until the district attorney came over.

"Congrats, Bomber," Web said. "I didn't think you'd get this one."

Bomber looked up with a rueful smile, as though he had been confident all along, but he said, "You aren't the only one. Thanks."

Joan came up to give me a hug and whispered in my ear, "In gut we trust." Then a swarm of well wishers came to congratulate Melissa, who was gracious to a fault. Among the gaggle were Henry Ziggenfoos and Foster Teague. Fingers Sulwip had been taken back to jail.

"Does this mean I'm free?" Melissa asked Bomber. "I can just...go?"

"Yes it does, my dear. Congratulations, Godspeed."

"Oh, thank you," she said throwing her arms around him, causing Bomber the pained expression he always got at the slightest public intimacy. "*You* did it," she said, loosening her grip and standing back to look in his eye. "I will forever be grateful."

Bomber patted her arm, "Wait with your unbounded gratitude until you get my bill."

That was good for a tension-easing laugh. Though the verdict had been rendered, there was still tension, as though we may have won without really deserving to.

Melissa was engulfed in the sea of her well wishers, and they floated out of the courtroom.

As we gathered our papers, Bomber said, "Good job with the scenarios."

"Thanks," I said. "Have a favorite?"

He passed the back of his hand under his nose. "Foster did the lying. I'd like to see him in there somewhere." So we went out to the hall where jurors traditionally gather to tell the attorneys how they arrived at their decisions.

It was, naturally enough, the man we feared most, Axel Johnson, the one Bomber had mercilessly questioned while he was selecting the jury from this impossible pool, who presented himself as their spokesman.

"Came down to this, Bomber," he said with a smile of self-importance, "we didn't believe she could do it. The evidence wasn't that important. I think if we all *saw* her do it the verdict'd be the same. And if we were wrong," he shrugged his beefy shoulders, "he had it coming. I mean, Easy was no great loss to society. We all said she suffered enough. Put her back to work at the things she does best—helping people."

On our way to the cars, Joan smiled her Cheshire cat smile and got in another dig: "Trust in gut."

"Yeah," I said, "if it's yours."

The three of us were on the sidewalk, and I don't think Bomber could still grasp what had happened when we saw at the corner, waiting for the light to change, our client and a man. They were holding hands. It didn't take long for us to recognize the man. It was Foster Teague. Just before the light changed, he leaned over and planted a quick, yet passionate kiss on Melissa's lips.

Bomber looked at me.

I looked at him.

I looked away.

I looked back. He was still looking at me.

Our pace slowed to a morose crawl. Just as we reached where the Bentley was parked, and we said congratulations to Bomber and goodbye, Teague's Mercedes came tooling by with the proprietor at the wheel and Melissa in the passenger seat.

They didn't see us. They had eyes only for each other.

Bomber watched them go, and shook his head. "The mind of a man," he said, "is never more wonderful than when it tricks us."

ALLEN A. KNOLL, PUBLISHERS
Established 1989

We are a small press located in Santa Barbara, Ca,
specializing in
books for intelligent people who read for fun.

Please visit our website at www.knollpublishers.com
for a complete catalog, scintilating sample chapters,
in depth interviews, and thought-provoking
reading guides.

Or call (800) 777-7623 to receive a catalog and/or be
kept informed of new releases.